A.A. LEWIS

Copyright © 2023 A.A. Lewis

All rights reserved. No part of this book may be reproduced in any form or by any electronic or mechanical means, including information storage and retrieval systems, without permission in writing from the publisher, except by reviewers, who may quote brief passages in a review.

The characters and events contained in this book are fictitious. Any similarities to real persons, living or dead and or events are coincidental and not intended by the author.

Credits for cover design and images by Grafiz_Designs
Editor-Rosemary Dugan

Printed in the United States of America

Published by D & S Publishing
Kalamazoo, MI 49009
lewisaa716@gmail.com

"A Good Man will want you to shine. He will love you in your purest imperfect state. He will honor you with his words and in his deeds. His goal will be to make you smile and to offer protection from the outside world. A Good Man will allow you to be vulnerable without fear of being exposed. His touch will comfort and his kisses a source of healing."

- A. A. Lewis

ACKNOWLEDGEMENTS

To The Readers
Thank you for supporting me through the good times and bad. Your love, support, and encouragement during my time of rest and healing mean the world to me. I hope this book brings you the drama, sophistication, and satisfaction that you have come to expect from my work. Thank you for sticking with me and continuing this journey with me. Blessings to you all. Happy reading!

To My Family
The past three years have not been easy, but like everything else, the Lewis household has endured, and this too shall pass. Thank you for allowing me to take it easy. I appreciate everyone's willingness to pitch in, so I could remove my superhero cape and be human. The love and attention you all have shown me give me hope that whatever I am going through mentally, physically, and emotionally, I have your full, unwavering support. I know I am not the easiest person to please, but deep down, my gratitude sings your praises. Darryl, Kyon, and Ahmir, I love you more than words and actions can express. Thank you.

To Darryl
You are book bae goals. I didn't say you were perfect, but you're just right for me. Thank you for being my support system, my voice of reason, and my hype man. Your love keeps me pushing forward when it's so easy to give up. And now that I get to share this creative space with you, I know it truly is #myhustlehisgrind. Twenty-five years and we are still together. Blessings.

To My Sister Rose
A million thank yous could never be enough. I appreciate you for always being there for me, no questions asked. Love you always.

Table of Contents

Meet The Characters 9
Chapter One 20
Chapter Two 25
Chapter Three 32
Chapter Four 41
Chapter Five 48
Chapter Six 54
Chapter Seven 62
Chapter Eight 66
Chapter Nine 74
Chapter Ten 81
Chapter Eleven 92
Chapter Twelve 99
Chapter Thirteen 102
Chapter Fourteen 109
Chapter Fifteen 113
Chapter Sixteen 118
Chapter Seventeen 126
Chapter Eighteen 132
Chapter Nineteen 135
Chapter Twenty 139

Chapter Twenty-One	146
Chapter Twenty-Two	149
Chapter Twenty-Three	156
Chapter Twenty-Four	162
Chapter Twenty-Five	166
Chapter Twenty-Six	172
Chapter Twenty-Seven	176
Chapter Twenty-Eight	186
Chapter Twenty-Nine	192
Chapter Thirty	195
Chapter Thirty-One	204
Chapter Thirty-Two	210
Chapter Thirty-Three	213
Chapter Thirty-Four	216
Chapter Thirty-Five	221
Chapter Thirty-Six	226
Chapter Thirty-Seven	230
Epilogue	238
About The Author	244

MEET THE CHARACTERS

DeShawn Baugh

CHAPTER ONE

"Man, as soon as I get home I'mma start dinner and run the bath water for my lady." I confessed to Greg.

"Fool, she got you whipped like some Babyface shit," he joked.

"Call it what you want, but I would rather be at home booed up with my lady than roaming these tired ass streets any day. At some point in your life, man, you're going to want something other than the flavor of the day. Besides, you're getting too old for the club scene. Them young girls gonna kill your ass." I said, laughing out loud.

"Well, call me crazy, because I'm not ready for that monogamy shit. I'm waiting for the Commodore lady. You know, the bad bitch with 36-24-36," he said as he made the hourglass shape with his hands. I just shook my head. The garbage truck stopped at the next house on our route. We both jumped off and cleared the next few houses as we continued our banter. I've known guys like Greg my whole life. Guys that were always chasing after the elusive perfect girl. It didn't matter how bad their current girl was, they always thought there was something better out there. Even Eddie Murphy's character in Boomerang found out the hard way about chasing after something that doesn't really exist.

Now, that's not to say that there aren't some bad chicks out there. Lord knows I had my share. All I'm saying is, if you find a diamond, ain't no need to keep digging. Hell, if you brush off that diamond and take care of it, who's to say it won't shine brighter than anything you ever seen or become more valuable with time? Greg and most of the dudes I knew cannot see the beauty of women. I mean the genuine beauty. They were too busy looking at the superficial things and not digging deeper to see the real charm they possessed. I promised myself the moment the right lady came into my world, I would hold on to her with both hands. So, the moment Evette Monique Watts crossed my path, I did that and more.

"So, I take it you're not coming out with the rest of us tonight?" Shawn, the driver, yelled out the window of the front of the truck.

"Naw, man. But y'all can have a round on me." I said, confirming my decision to keep to my plans with Evette. I saw Mike shaking his head in disbelief. Greg and I cleared the rest of the street. This was our last run for the day. We had been at it since five this morning. It was a full twelve-hour shift. I won't complain. Lord knows it was better than no job at all or worse, those days I spent locked up. No, it wasn't the cash I was used to flashing in my youth, but an honest day's work and legit pay beat not having my freedom any day. Greg and I tapped the truck to signal we were done. We hung on the back of the truck as we coasted through the inner-city blocks heading back downtown to the truck depot. The cool fall air had me thinking of Evette's warm body. Fuck these niggas! Ain't no way they could win over an evening with my lady, I thought to myself as we pulled into the truck yard, signaling the end of our shift.

The truck came to a complete stop, and Greg and I jumped off the back. I walked over to the driver's side window. Mike handed me my lunch box and jacket.

"Man, last chance," he said, gesturing for me to come and hang out with him and the fellas. I just shook my head no as Greg climbed in the truck.

"Fuck him and his whip appeal ass. More honeys for us," Greg laughed.

"Alright fellas. I'll see yall on Monday. They rode off to park the truck as I yelled. I walked over to the employee dock. I searched for my time card, stood in line with the rest of the workers, and clocked out. I walked towards my black Ford F150 truck, jumped in, and drove off. There was a woman I needed to see and a date I had to prepare for.

When I received a text from Evette, I was almost done cooking dinner.

> **Evette-**
> Hey Baby, I'm out with the girls. I'll be home later.

Hesitating, I waited to respond. I can't say I wasn't disappointed. But she was free to do what she wanted to. If she needed time out with her girls, then I needed to respect that. Evette was a few years younger than me. She was a college educated woman. Independent, strong career, and beautiful. She differed from any women that I had dated prior to her.

Let me clarify: Evette was kind and loving. She was comfortable with me and my past. She accepted me for who I was, my rough edges and all. I mean, I was a street dude. I was good at math, primarily because of selling bricks. You better know how to count on a whim or your ass will be taken advantage of real quick. Last thing you want is to come up short. I graduated high school, but the thought of attending college never entered my mind, even though my grades were stellar. My school counselor thought I could get a scholarship and encouraged me to apply. Another four years of school was no match for the lure of the streets. The fast money, cars, and girls was all a young man like myself was interested in. So, I was smart. I had a little book knowledge and a lot of street sense. I knew enough to think before I answered Evette's text.

Me–
No worries, sexy lady. I'll be here when you return.

She heart emoji me back. I guess it was dinner for one tonight. Grabbing my plate, I dug in. I flipped through the cable channels. There was a basketball game on. Chicago and Detroit were playing. Although I liked football more, I had that playing in the background to keep me company. After dinner, I cleaned the kitchen. I fixed Evette a plate of food and left it on the counter for her. Making myself comfortable on the couch, I attempted to watch the game. It had been some time since I'd actually watched a basketball game and I found myself lost. Most of the players were foreign to me. The game had changed so much since I was a kid. I recognized a few names only because their father's played in the league when I was growing up. Before long, I drifted off to sleep.

I woke up at one in the morning to the blaring sounds of the television. The infomercial was announcing the reduction in the price of some cookware set as I reached for the remote and turned the television off. The house was empty. I noticed Evette's plate was still on the kitchen counter. I grabbed it and placed it in the refrigerator as I headed off to the bedroom. Before laying down, I sent Evette a text.

Me-
Hey baby, I just want to make sure you're good?

Within seconds, she responded.

Evette-
Hey baby, yeah. Still out with the girls. Be home soon.

With that, I rested my tired head down for the night, not before laughing to myself. If Greg and Mike knew I got stood up for a girls' night out, they would never let me live this down. Good thing I wasn't one of those dudes that had to run their mouth about everything that happened between them and their girl. I considered myself too mature for playing childish games. Besides, Evette was a whole ass woman with needs outside of what we had going on. If she wanted to hang out with her girls, I was cool with that. I'll be right here waiting for her to return. If I'm lucky, she might be a little tipsy and wanna do something to me. Just the thought of her and her curves made my manhood jump. I gripped him and said, " Hold on, man. Baby girl will be home soon enough." I shook my head to rid myself of the thoughts of what I wanted to do to her. Last thing I needed was my dick on swole.

CHAPTER TWO

"Who was that?" Sharmaine asked, rolling her eyes.

"You know good and damn well who it was. It was the felon," Bridgett clowned.

"Y'all need to stop it. At least I have a man to check on me and make sure I'm ok." I clapped back.

"You have a point. But girl.." Bridgette said as she took a sip of her cocktail.

"Girl what?" I asked.

"That nigga is a felon. I'm just saying I think you could do so much better." Bridgette answered.

"For crying out loud, he's a garbage man. So he makes like what, minimum wage?" Sharmaine chimed in, sounding disgusted.

"For your information, he makes over fifty thousand." I said, trying to defend my man.

"And you make triple that. So tell me, is the dick really that good that you would lower your standards?" Sharmaine asked.

"Shidd, she didn't just lower her standards, she straight went to the gutter literally. That dick must be good and dirty," Bridgette laughed, causing both of us to join in.

Y'all need to stop it. I don't see either of you bitches getting dick on the regular, let alone a man in sight. Deshawn is a good guy. Can both of you stop being so judgmental? If y'all were really my friends, you would be happy for me. Besides, I stuck by your sorry asses through a lot worse. Lord knows y'all dated some characters. Some that should be felons, Sharmaine." I said, annoyed.

"Evette, you're right. But damn. A garbage man." Bridgette said, laughing.

"Fuck you," I said, laughing.

We were seated at the perfect table at the bar. On Fridays, there was a live band that played 90's R & B covers. It was grown people shit. The vibe was really cool. It was the ideal end of a hectic week. Plus, I loved spending time with my girls. Bridgette, Sharmaine, and I were college friends. They were my girls from way back. We had been there for each other through thick and thin. I knew they had my best interest at heart and only spoke up because they cared. But I wish they saw what I see in Deshawn. Everything was fine when they first saw him. Hell, they even wanted to get with him. And who could blame them?

Deshawn was fine as hell. His low tapered waves and well-trimmed beard initially caught my attention. I loved a guy with a beard. But then he stood up and started walking toward our table. He stood about six feet two inches, and his athletic build filled out his tailored suit just enough to peak every girl's interest that night. To my surprise, he asked me to dance. I didn't know what to say. So, I declined. I mean, why would he want to dance with me when Brigette and Sharmaine looked more like his type of girl? He smiled and walked back over to the group of men he was with. For the rest of the night, I watched as girls approached him and he smiled and would occasionally shake his head no.

By the end of the night, we met up again as we were existing the club. He gave me his number and said he hoped I would call. I blushed as he kissed my hand and walked away, not before he turned around and smiled at me one last time. The scent of his cologne lived rent free in my nostrils for the next week until I finally mustered up the courage to call him. He didn't answer, and I was relieved. I wasn't even sure what I was going to say. Before the final beep to leave, a message sounded. I hung up the phone. Within a few minutes, my cell phone rang. It was the same number I dialed. I answered it, not thinking.

"Hello Ms. Lady. I was starting to think you weren't going to call me." The strong masculine voice said.

"Hello." I responded, sounding like a schoolgirl.

"So, tell me your name, beautiful." He asked.

"Evette. Evette Watts. And you are?" I quizzed.

"Deshawn Baugh." He replied. There was an infinitesimal pause. Then he continued, " So Evette, tell me about your day."

"You really don't want to know that." I said.

"Yes, I do. I wanna know that and so much more. But I'll settle on knowing how your day went, so I can figure out what I can do to make it better." He responded, causing my panties to become moist. I gasped for air as I thought of what to say next. "Evette, are you still there?" he asked.

"Yes, I'm here." I paused as I proceeded to tell him about my day. Before I knew it, we had been on the phone for three hours. We talked about life, current events and nothing at all. He made me laugh and blush. It had been a while since I felt so free with someone. I liked it. So much so that I accepted his invitation to dinner.

One date led to another, and seven months later we were still together. Deshawn checked off so many of the attributes in a man I had prayed for. All except for being a felon and not making six figures. He would be perfect if we could just subtract those two items from his record. Bridgette and Sharmaine weren't that easily swayed when I told them we were dating. Then, when they found out about his past, they quickly dismissed him. They even said we wouldn't last and here we were still together.

"Girl, please tell me you not thinking about that negro?" Bridgette joked.

"Y'all just don't understand." I said, smiling just thinking about all the things Deshawn does for me.

" We already know he got you dickmatized, because it sure ain't the money." Sharmaine joked.

"Ok enough. On that note, I'm out." I grabbed my purse and coat.

"No, don't go. We'll behave ourselves. Promise," Bridgette tried to reassure me. It was too late. I had heard enough insults for one evening. It was well past two in the morning. Unlike them, I had a man at home waiting for me. They kept me out later than I had planned. I gave them both kisses on the cheek.

"I'll text you bitches when I get home." I yelled out over the music playing as I headed toward the front door. My car was parked right across the street in front of the club. I was good friends with the bouncer. Curtis walked me out to my car and watched me drive off.

I pulled into my condominium parking garage and placed my car in my assigned spot. Immediately, I took the elevator up to the seventh floor. I staggered my way to my door as I texted the girls that I made it home. Upon entering the front door, a trail of rose petals and the fresh flowers in the vase on the hallway table greeted me. The note beside the vase said, "Wake me when you get in." Damn. I fucked up. Staying out all night with Bridgette and Sharmaine was not part of the plan. I walked the pathway of rose petals as they led me into the bedroom. He had the house smelling warm and cozy. I took a quick look and saw Deshawn peacefully resting. I slowly closed the bedroom door and went the other way.

I tossed my purse and coat onto the dining room table. I made my way over to the fridge. My stomach was growling. All that drinking had me wishing I had eaten something earlier. I saw the plate of food Deshawn left for me. In my drunken state, I didn't even heat the food up. I grabbed a fork from the kitchen drawer and dug in. Deshawn was an excellent cook. He spoiled me with his good home cooking. And you know it's good if you can eat it cold or the next day and it tastes even better. I was just about done with my plate when I heard the bedroom door open.

"Did I wake you, baby?," I asked.

"No. You know I can't sleep right without you by my side," Deshawn stated as he kissed my cheek. "I see you found your plate.,"

"Ooh baby, it was so good. Boy, you need to be on Top Chef." I said, not realizing I was that hungry.

"Thank you, sweetheart," he replied, laughing.

"What's so funny?," I questioned.

"You are so cute when you're drunk." Deshawn stated.

"I know. I wasn't supposed to stay out this late. "Confession time. I really wanted to come home to you."

"And you did. I hope you had fun with your girls," Deshawn commented as he removed my heels from my feet.

" Yass baby, that feels so good." I whispered, as he massaged my feet. The way Deshawn touched me was so gentle. You would think that his hands would be callus and rough from the work he did, but they weren't. His hands were soft, and he kept them manicured. His hands made their way up my thighs as I sunk deep into the barstool at the kitchen island. Deshawn kissed every inch of my legs before taking my hand and leading me into the bedroom ensuite.

Deshawn prepared a fresh bath for me. He knew how much I loved bathing in my extra-large soaking tub that overlooked the city lights of downtown. He watched me as I undressed. I was still shy when it came to him viewing my body. His body was so well toned and my body was well just there. My stretch marks told my struggle with my weight. I was self-conscience about my curves and often wondered why Deshawn loved my body so much. I guess I was taking too long over thinking my appearance, that I didn't notice that Deshawn was now naked and assisted me. His chiseled body held my softness in his arms as we sank into the hot water of the tub.

I rested my body against Deshawn as he gingerly washed my body. With every touch, my body craved him. He felt so good as the soapy wash cloth glided over my curves. I laid on him as the water rocked back and forth between us from the slight movements of his hands.
"You know I got a thing for you, girl," he whispered in my ear.
I just smirked. "Sure you do. I'm not sure why you do," I uttered softly, spilling my private thoughts out loud.

"Well, for starters, you're intelligent. You're sexy, confident, and classy. You make me smile and you appreciate me. You don't try to change me. Plus, you got that wet, wet just like I like it." He whispered as he kissed my neck. "Does that answer your question?" he continued.

"Yes" I sighed softly. We sat there in the tub for a few minutes. Deshawn allowed me to just relax as the dark skies of the city skyline bounced off the tinted bathroom window. The flickering of the candle wick was the only visible light in the room. We sat there in silence, just enjoying the moment.

By the time we were done, Deshawn had dried my body off and massaged some mango body butter all over my voluptuous body. He escorted me to the bed and tucked me in. The last thing I remember was falling asleep in his arms. I wished I had the courage to jump his bone. It would have been the perfect time for me to show him just how much I appreciated him. But my confidence was only as strong as the last shot I had, and that was two hours ago. My high had worn off, and I was tired as fuck. I told myself next time I'm going to do it as sleep crept over me and the weight of my eyelids forced me to succumb to the early morning hours.

CHAPTER THREE

I woke up early the next morning. Evette was sleeping peacefully. It was Saturday. My body begged for a good workout. I slipped on my compression tights and a pair of joggers. I opted for my Black AF sweatshirt over my basic black wife beater tee. The last thing I needed was my all-black Nike Huaraches, and I was all set. My gym bag was by the front door. The pre-made protein shake was ice cold as I grabbed it from the refrigerator. With my keys in hand, I double checked to make sure I had everything I needed to start my day off right. Stepping out into the brisk fall morning was the jolt of energy I needed. My car was parked right next to Evette's Cream BMW XB7. The truck turned on and I pulled out of the parking garage. I made a sharp right on to the one-way street and headed toward the gym.

The parking lot was scarcely populated. I spotted the usual cars that are normally present for this time of day. Exercising at six in the morning on the weekend allowed me to start my day off right. Plus, the gym wasn't as crowded during this time. I scanned my phone at the check-in kiosk as the young lady greet me. I smiled and walked toward the men's changing room. Opening my assigned locker, I placed my bag and sweatpants in there, but not before taking my towel, Beats headset and hand wraps out.

There was no way I could get a good workout in without either of these items. Spinning off my combination on the lock, I closed the locker and walked onto the gym floor.

At first, I warmed up by doing some cardio. Once the blood was flowing well, it was time to put some work in. From my arms to my core, I was getting it in. My playlist of nineties rap music was blasting in my ear and had me feeling hype. I was working up a good sweat, when I stopped to get a drink of water from the water fountain. There were a few ladies in front of me that giggled and seemed to know each other from their body language. I couldn't hear their conversation. The music from my headset was screaming, and my mind was focused on my next set of reps. One of the young girls tapped me on my arm just as I was going to take a sip of water.

I removed my ear buds just in time to hear the last few words she said.

"... some water?"

"My apologies. I had my ear buds in and didn't hear what you said," I stated.

"Oh, I was just wondering why you don't have a water bottle. I would be more than happy to share my water with you." She replied, smiling as her girls giggled from a distance.

"Thank you, sweetheart, but I'm good," I said, bending down to take another sip.

"Well, if you ever get tired of drinking from the fountain, I'll be here." She commented.

I smiled and shook my head as I turned to walk back to my workout. I had to hand it to women today. They were not afraid to go after what they wanted. This was a change from most women I knew back in the day. The independent women wasted no time letting men know what they wanted or how they wanted it. But me, I was a born hunter. While it was cute and quite an ego boost to have woman come up to me and try to run game, I preferred to be the pursuer. Most men, any real man, did. I know times have changed, but the last thing I wanted was for some cutie to approach me, talking about some "slim-thick". That shit didn't sound right or look ok to me. But I had to hand it to ole girl, she was fine and so were her friends. Luckily for me, all I came here for was a good workout. Anything else I had waiting at home for me.

I finished my last set of leg presses and then ran five miles on the treadmill before packing up and heading back to Evette's house. As soon as I arrived, I went downstairs to the mail room and collected her mail and a few boxes that had been delivered to her. Charles, the condo attendant, was stationed at the front desk. He was a cool older guy. I had become fond of him. He reminded me of that cool uncle we all had that was a player back in their prime. Let Charles tell it, he still was. I stopped to chat with him for a moment and handed him a cup of coffee and his favorite bagel from the pastry shop down the street. This had become our weekly ritual. Plus, he gave me the rundown on everything that was going on in these streets. We dapped each other up before I headed up to the seventh floor.

Evette's condo covered a fourth of the floor. She had the right corner unit that overlooked the downtown city skyline. I knew this place cost a pretty penny. Hell, it had everything you could ever need on the first floor of the building, including a mini grocery store. Evette tried to get me to use the gym facilities on the second floor, but there was something about being around non-melanated people in my free time that turned me off. No disrespect, but Lord knows I spent three years listening to the man give me orders. Even today, everything I did was controlled by someone who did not look like me. The last thing I needed was to be minding my own black business exercising and have one of them approach me wrong. I would never want that backlash to fall on Evette. So it was best I stick to my routine and comfort zone.

I dropped off the mail and boxes in the kitchen. My standard Saturday goods were placed on the serving tray I prepared. I grabbed Evette a cup of espresso from her favorite neighborhood spot. I had bagels and croissants from the pastry shop and a fresh stem flower for my lady. Fresh fruit and an assortment of jams and bacon finished my presentation. I hopped in the shower and rinsed off the remnants of my morning. Wrapping the towel around my waist, I went to the kitchen to get the morning delights on the tray. I walked back into the bedroom to find Evette still sleeping peacefully. I sat the tray down on my side of the bed. Walking over to her side of the bed. I bent down to kiss her good morning.

"Good morning, sleeping beauty." I stated as her eyes opened. There was nothing like her smile. It was pure and sincere. She rubbed her eyes before speaking.

"What time is it, Deshawn?" she asked.

"It's eight-thirty." I replied.

"Did you already go workout?" she questioned.

"Yup, and I got all your favorites." I said, pointing at the delicious array of breakfast goods on the wooden tray.

"Even the chocolate filled croissants?" she whimpered.

"Especially the chocolate filled croissants." I smiled as I lifted the tray up and placed it in the middle of the bed so that she could dig in. I turned the television on and allowed the morning news to play in the background. When I was locked up, I became interested in current events and politics. It's amazing what interests you once your civil liberties get taken away. The news was one of the few outlets I had to the outside world. That and the many books in the library. I vowed that if I was ever given a second chance, I wouldn't take any of my freedoms for granted. I sat there while Evette munched down on the breakfast I prepared.

"You're not going to eat?" she asked.

"No, baby. I had a protein shake and a banana. You enjoy it." I said.

"What the fuck!? You think I'm about to eat this shit by myself?" She huffed pushing the tray away, annoyed.

"Yo, slow down, baby. What's the issue?" I asked, questioning the change in her gratitude.

"Why would you buy all of this if you're not going to join me? I'm already fat. I don't need you treating me like a fat girl!" She screamed.

'Whoa. First lower your voice, ma. Now, I brought you your favorite items, not because I think you're fat, but because I knew you would appreciate them. If you would rather me do something different, tell me. If you eating alone bothers you, say less. I can wait until I get home from the gym to have my shake and fruit. But reacting like this.. this isn't it, ma," I calmly said. Evette huffed and puffed while processing what I had told her. I removed the tray off the bed and sat it on the dresser. I then walked over to Evette and sat down beside her. There was a moment of silence before I kissed her lips. That seemed to soften for the moment as her facial muscles eased up. Her pouting became puckers as she kissed me back.

Like clockwork, my manhood instantly became erect at the thought of being inside Evette. The passion between us had escalated to full body caressing. My towel had unraveled and fallen off, leaving me exposed. Evette saw this as an opportunity to caress my swollen meat. First with her hands and then with her tongue. My eyes stayed focused on her as she worked all erect ten inches of me in and out of her mouth. It was warm and wet as she sucked on me. Her steady jerks and pulls teased me like nothing I had experienced before. The way she fondled my scrotum with one hand and stroked my shaft simultaneously showed me just how efficient Evette was in handling her business. She wasn't scared of my size and didn't back down from the challenge of taking me whole down her hot throat. The sounds that she made as she enjoyed me set me off. I was ready for the main attraction, her.

Slowly, I pulled away from Evette's grasp. My hard dick was in my hands. I smiled as I looked down at Evette as she licked her lips. Quickly grabbing both her legs, pulling her to the edge of the bed. I reached down in a deep squat formation, cuffed her ass and lifted her above my waist. With both legs dangling over my arms, I lowered Evette down until my member met her opening. Gently, I entered her as she sighed.

"Put me down," she whispered.

I grinned at her command and shook my head no as I entered her again and again. I lifted and lowered her with accuracy as she held on to my neck. Her softness covered me like a perfectly quilted covering. It was tight and wet. Soaking wet. It was easy for me to get lost in her sweetness as oceans of juices collided with me when I entered her. The tip of my dick tingled every time I plunged deeper and deeper into her walls. I grunted as she moaned and called out my name.

"Don't drop me," she cried out.

"I have no intentions of letting you go. The only thing I'm going to do is make you feel good." I said, as I pumped her even harder. "Now let me do my job, so I can fuck you right," I grunted.

My message must have been received and welcomed because within minutes, Evette was cumming all over my deep strokes. Her sloppy wetness caused me to slip in and out of her uncontrollably. This meant only one thing: I needed to clean her up. I pulled out of Evette's hot creamy dam and carried her to the bed. With care, I laid her down and positioned myself between her thighs to begin kissing my way to the center of her womanhood. I licked my way to her energy source and allowed my tongue to dance on her clit until she showered me with love. She tasted like honey; raw sweet honey and I was addicted. I could hear her screams for me to stop, but my compulsion to conquer my addiction propelled me further into her wet, energized center until I suffocated from her juices.

When I finally came up for air, Evette's juices dripped from my beard like a fresh rain downpour. I could smell her scent all over my face, and I loved it. The smile on her face and the tired look in her eyes told me I was on the right road to ease whatever stress she had carried over into the weekend. My manhood was on high alert as I flipped Evette's curvy body over. She immediately arched her back into a deep slope, causing her ass to tilt high in the air. With one powerful slap, I greeted her kind gesture before I braced myself to enter her again. Her ass shook as she twerked it on me. I rode every wave of excitement as she bounced back on me. Evette was curvier than most girls I had dated, but she took all of me without so much as a whimper. I loved that she fucked me back and didn't allow my size or hers to get in the way of us loving on each other.

Evette threw that ass back on me, swallowing up my dick. The way her coochie lips wrapped around the tip of my head and sucked me in repeatedly caused me to lose control and she knew it. I refused to give in and quickly switched up my pace. I hit that fat ass and swung my dick from side to side, touching the inner walls of her lady parts. That slight curve of my shaft must have touched a sensitive spot because she screamed out loud and cussed my name to god. I knew I had her once she started speaking in tongues. I knew I laid one hell of a pipe, but Evette's pussy was some of the best shit I had slid into. And I had my fair share of cooch.

I flipped her full body over and kissed my way back into her. With her legs wrapped around my neck, I pounded her slit until her well had dried up. All I heard was Evette's moans and the rest for me to give it to her. With her encouragement to go on, I headed back down between her thighs and massaged her energy source until her juices flowed freely. Sliding my hard dick back into her as she lay on the bed face up, I licked her round titties as she sucked her juices off my beard. It turned me on. I loved it when she sucked my tongue and beard after I dove deep into her love. I believed if a woman wouldn't at least suck your fingers after they had been inside her, that was one clue that I shouldn't be tasting her either. Evette was no stranger to the way she tasted and on occasions had even licked my johnson clean after cumming on me. It was an instant turn on and watching her savor her juice set off a chain reaction in me as my strides quickened; her moans intensified and the sweet images of her played out in real time caused me to explode deep within her walls. "Damn Evette," I uttered as her lips tightened from the strength of her Kegel muscles.

I rested on top of Evette. The warmth of her body felt like home as our heartbeats synchronized. I know it had only been seven months, but Evette was the woman for me. The only woman I wanted to spend the rest of my life with. It was moments like this that made me regret not finding her sooner. But I thank the Lord every day that he brought her into my life. I was falling head over heels for her. So much so that I was thinking of hanging up my jersey for her. It was that serious. I knew she wanted to take things slow, but I had already done my dirt. There wasn't anything left for me out in these streets. I was a grown man with grown man needs and Evette checked off everything I wanted in a partner. She was the real deal. I just needed to make sure she knew that and make my move, I thought to myself as my head rested on her breasts and we dozed off for a mid-day nap.

CHAPTER FOUR

After waking up from our morning fun, Deshawn and I showered and made time for a quickie before finally getting it together and heading out for some Saturday errands. We needed to go grocery shopping and a few other places. Plus, tonight we were hanging out with a few of his friends. Deshawn had a few friends that were in long-term relationships who we hung out with occasionally. I liked Paul and his girlfriend, Anita. Then there were Tim and Tweet. I loved their energy. The two of them were so wild and crazy. Tweet reminded me of me and my girls. It was always a good time when we got together and a refreshing exchange from hanging with my single friends. None of them had anything but positive things to say about Deshawn. I loved them for that and the support they gave our relationship.

I allowed Deshawn to drive my car whenever we were together. It gave me a chance to surf social media. He was the only man I had ever allowed to have keys to my place and drive my car. Not that I didn't trust any of the other guys I dated, Deshawn and I just always seemed to be together. He never wanted me to "just meet him somewhere". He would pick me up, open doors, and make sure I felt safe. And he was succeeding. He was a true gentleman. Not to mention the way he loved me. I didn't think I would ever get my hair to act right after what he did to me this morning. That man knew he laid the pipe with accuracy. It was true, I was dickmatized. But more than that, Deshawn treated me like gold. He knew exactly what to say and do to keep me happy. It often made me feel like he had an angle because there just couldn't be a man this good still left in the world. I wanted to let my guard down with him completely, but my past experiences with men I thought loved me wouldn't allow me to. But damnit, he put up a good fight, so why shouldn't I just give in to my heart?

Deshawn and I first went to this boutique I wanted to visit. They had just opened up and they carried clothing in all sizes. Deshawn parked the car, walked around to the passenger side door and opened it for me. He lent me his hand to assist me out of the car and closed the door behind me. I heard the "beep beep" sound of the security device on the car notifying me that I had locked the doors as we walked toward the store. Deshawn walked on the outer side of the sidewalk as we held hands. It was one of those Indian summer days where it was warm enough for long sleeves but not cold enough for a full coat. I was wearing a full-length navy-blue sweater cardigan with a white tank top, form fitting jeans and heels. Deshawn matched my outfit as he complimented my blue sweater with his printed blue button-down shirt, gray sweater jacket, and jeans. His ink-colored Wallaby's set off his outfit just right.

As the wind blew, I could smell Deshawn's cologne leaving a trail of his whereabouts. He smiled at me as he opened the door of the boutique. I waltzed right in as our presence alerted the workers that we were there.

"Hello, welcome," a friendly lady spoke.

"Hello" Deshawn and I spoke in unison.

"Baby, are you looking for something special?" he asked as we strolled through the store.

"No, I just wanted to see what they offered." I replied as I touch a few items that caught my eye. Deshawn followed closely behind me. We whispered to each other about a few of the items. He would hold something up he liked and showed me, and I would do the same. We each had a few items in our hands. Deshawn had obliviously assumed that I wanted his help picking out clothes. He insisted I try on the items he liked. I was hesitant. I mean, what man willingly goes shopping with their girl and pics out outfits for them? He didn't even know my size. I rolled my eyes at him, annoyed he would try to embarrass me by picking up stuff that I just knew would never look good on me. One of the store employees approached us and asked if she could start a dressing room for me. I shook my head and answered, "Yes, please."

I walked into the dressing room, while Deshawn took a seat on the sofa that was in front of the entrance to the fitting area.

"Baby, I wanna see you in the clothes I picked out," he yelled out loud for everyone to hear. It wasn't bad enough that I wasn't comfortable with him choosing items for me, but now he wanted me to model these items for him. My anxiety kicked in. I took a deep breath and just tried on the items I picked out first. As I tried on the items, I was impressed at how they accentuated my curves. I looked banging in them. It was definitely the pick me up I needed. There was a knock at the fitting room door. It was the store employee.

"Hi, Evette, right?"

"Yes" I questioned.

"Your boyfriend asked me to bring these back to you. Let me know if we need to get different sizes." She stated. As she hung the items on the hook for me. She closed the door behind her as she smile and said, " You look incredible in those jeans." I smiled back and thanked her.

I just know he didn't hand her some lingerie. The fact that he would even suggest I model this in public was disgusting to me. I was not some thirsty thot. There was no way I was going out there in this for the world to see. I sucked my teeth as I thumbed through Deshawn's picks. I decided to just try on the dress he picked out and the skirt. Everything else was a no.

To my surprise, the dress looked gorgeous on me. He got lucky with the size, plus the dress had some stretch to it. The off-shoulder dress hugged my curves just right. I loved the teal color and the draped back. From all the angles, I looked good. I decided after a few moments to walk out to show Deshawn, who was patiently waiting on the couch.

"Umm." I said, clearing my throat to get his attention. I made a quick turn so that he could see. I loved the smile that plastered across his face. He looked pleased at what he saw.

"Damn Baby! You wearing the hell out of that dress? I want to see more. If they all look like that, I'm buying it all," he proclaimed.

"You don't have to do that. Besides, this store is on the expensive side." I joked. But Deshawn paid me no attention. I waved goodbye and went back into the dressing room. The attention he gave me encouraged me to try on the rest of the items he picked up, minus the lingerie. Shit, everything that Deshawn had chosen for me looked great on my body. I was impressed with his taste and the fact that he picked the right sizes for me. I went back out there with all the confidence I had and modeled each item for him. He loved it and so did I.

"Are you going to show me the other items?" he asked.

"You mean the lingerie?" I replied.

"Yes, that," he said. I looked at him like he was crazy. "Evette, I want to see it on you before I buy it," he continued.

"I told you that this stuff was expensive. You weren't listening to me." I stated, annoyed.

"I heard you the first time, and that is not what I asked," he said. We locked eyes, and I just shook my head and walked away. The nerve of him demanding something from me and he can't afford half the shit in this store I mumbled under my breath. I took the outfit off and stared at the lingerie on the hook. As I started trying on the first item, I shook my head. I stared at myself in the mirror. It wasn't bad. It wasn't bad at all. The strappy bra set actually looked good on me. The bra cup cuffed my breast just right and the boy shorts showed just enough cheek in the back. I stood there for a moment looking at myself, wondering why I was so self-conscious around Deshawn. My behavior with the other men I dated differed from this. I couldn't explain why I behaved the way I did when it came to him.

There was a knock at the fitting room door. I assumed it was the young lady who was assisting me. I opened the door. To my surprise, it was Deshawn. He stood there looking me over. He entered the narrow room and joined me. Deshawn positioned me to face the mirror so I could see myself. I saw my reflection. I noticed the way he looked at me as his hands traveled my body. He whispered, " You're the sexiest woman I know. I need you to know that. " He kissed me on my neck as he smiled at me before leaving the dressing room. My eyes met his reflection in the mirror as he left, and I began to cry, standing there in silence trying to see what he saw in me. I wanted to trust everything he said. I wanted to trust that Deshawn meant what he said. He was so handsome. So kind. How could someone like him really want me? I hated I felt this way.

I fixed my face, gathered my thoughts and the clothing from the hook and walked back out to the main showroom. Deshawn took hold of the hangers with one and held my hand with the other. He just smiled at me as he led me up to the register to checkout. There were additional items on the back counter that the sale lady rang up.

"Wait, I didn't ask for that," I spoke up.

"You're right. I did. Please continue," he instructed the young lady.

I stood there trying to figure out what he was doing. The sales clerk stated the total for the items. I grabbed my wallet out of my Chanel bag when Deshawn shot me a look I had not seen before. It stopped me dead in my tracks. He pulled out his wallet and handed the girl what appeared to be an American Express Black Card. She swiped the card, and the transaction was final. All two thousand and eight hundred dollars had cleared. Deshawn signed the electronic pad and grabbed the garment bags that held my purchased items. He thanked the staff for their help as we exited the boutique. Deshawn took my hand by force and guided me out of the store as he held the door open.

We walked back to the car in silence. He placed the items in the trunk of the car and escorted me to the passenger side of the car. I got in and buckled in my seat belt as he closed the door.

Deshawn got in the car. He didn't look at me the whole time we were in the car. Sirius XM played in the background as he drove. I noticed we were headed back toward my condo.

"I thought we were going to the grocery store," I said. Deshawn didn't say anything at first. I saw the vein in his temple flex. I knew that meant he was agitated. We just sat there in silence. Within minutes, we pulled into the condo's parking garage. Deshawn parked the car.

"I'm going to go to my place for a little while. I think it might be best if you take some time for yourself today. While you were in the dressing room, I called and made you an appointment to get a massage and your nails done at Sapphire Salon. I'll be back around seven to pick you up for tonight." Deshawn said as he leaned over to give me a kiss. Deshawn looked at me one last time before he exited the car. He walked around to the passenger side door and opened it so I could get out and into the driver's side seat. I watched as he climbed into his truck and drove away.

Fuck Evette! I screamed out loud. Don't mess this shit up, I thought to myself. I sat there in the car wanting to cry, but my pride wouldn't allow me to. I allowed myself to stew in my thoughts before I turned myself around. If he wanted to run off like a spoiled brat, then let him. I immediately phoned Sapphire Salon and added two more to my reservations. I called Bridgett and Sharmaine and told them I would be at their places in ten minutes, so get ready because we had a spa appointment.

CHAPTER FIVE

After leaving Evette in the parking garage, I headed to the barbershop. I needed to cool off. Evette's actions had me feeling some kind of way. I don't know what I needed to do to convince her I am that nigga. You would think that she knew that from my actions that I cared about her. Hell, I say it enough. And then her little smart remarks. If only she knew. Just thinking about what happened at the boutique had me fucked up. I tried to shrug it off or else it would mess up my whole day.

I pulled up in front of the barbershop just as Reginald was finishing up his last cut. Good thing he was family. I could slide right on in. I said hello to the rest of the fellas before sitting down in his chair. There was a steady flow of clientele coming and going out of the shop. Reginald or Reggie, as I called him, was one of the baddest barbers in town. His shop catered to a more mature group. There was jazz playing in the background. He offered whiskey and scotch to those who showed patronage to his establishment. It was definitely for grown men or father and son duals.

"Yo, what up fam?" Reggie asked as he brushed my hair.
"Nothing much, kid," I replied.
"You still with that thick chic? He asked.

"Man, why you checking for my lady?," I clowned.

"Naw, Shawn, your girl hella fine. I'm just saying, you sure you know what to do wit all that?," He responded, laughing.

Craig, the barber stationed next to him, laughed too.

"What you laughing at Craig?" I said in my best Friday voice.

"Man, you sure that you in the right lane with Shorty? I ain't never seen you with no big bone before. I mean, a girl like that needs a man like me. He laughed.

"Why the hell y'all niggas tryna pull rank on me for my girl?" I asked, laughing at their comments.

"Shawn, we ain't never seen you with no thick woman before. You normally go for them skinny girls." The other barber, Paul, chimed in. " You know the girls with just a touch of hips and thighs," he laughed, causing the rest of the guys to laugh, including me.

"Listen, when you find a good woman, size isn't a factor. E is just right for me. So sorry fellas y'all gonna be waiting a minute for me to fuck up. I'm playing for keeps with her." I stated.

"Say it ain't so," Reggie yelled out. "I just know the playa pimp himself isn't getting serious."

"Man. Let me tell you, when you find a good woman, you hold on to your good thing." I replied.

"It's like that, Shawn?" Paul asked.

'Word P. It's like that. Ms. Lady got me wanting to retire my jersey and shit. She definitely is special." I proclaimed.

"Damn Bro." Craig said. "If it's true, and you know, I'm happy for you, Shawn.,"

'Thanks, man." I said as he dapped me up.

"I better have a seat at this event when it go down," Paul said.

"No doubt. It's not every day that a man thinks about retiring from the game. When I do, you know it's a party." I laughed, and the fellas joined in.

I heard the buzzing and felt the vibrations of the clippers as Reggie glided them across my head. The truth was, I was ready to take the plunge. But it was moments like this morning that bothered me. In the past, that kind of behavior and disrespect from a girl I was dating would not be tolerated. I would have dropped her ass so fast. She would have gone back into the fitting room to get dressed and I would have peaked out. Thank goodness for growth and maturity. Evette was still young and I know that she's carrying baggage left over from previous relationships. When we started our journey as a couple and were getting to know each other, we discussed these things. But lately her actions have been speaking louder than her words and they both scream red flags and have me questioning if she really wants to be with me. None of this was something I'd ever discuss with my fellas. Barber shop talk was for shooting the breeze on sports, music, maybe even politics, but my personal relationship was not up for public debate. As men, we clown each other from time to time, but the respect I have for my woman won't allow me to discuss our private affairs with the masses.

"So everything is good?" Reggie asked as he spun the barber chair around. His comment snapped me out of my thoughts.

"Yeah, man. Evette is special. Real special." I said, as the smile on my face gave away my feelings.

"That's what I'm talking about." He said as he brushed me off with the neck duster. He edged me up and before I realized it, he completed my hair cut. Reggie spun me around in the chair and handed me the hand mirror to checkout my fresh cut. My waves were intact, and my edge up was sharp.

"Good lookin my G," I said as I dapped him up and paid for his services. I said my goodbyes to the rest of the crew and headed back out into the day.

I enjoyed spending my days and nights at Evette's condo, but there was nothing like me being in my space. Evette and I didn't technically live together. I had my home, and she had her condo. Occasionally she would spend the night with me, but mostly it was me venturing out to her place. Plus, I think Evette was more comfortable at her condo than she was in my neighborhood, even though I told her she was safe. I parked the car in the driveway. There were a few leaves in the front yard that I should attend to. I took pride in keeping the appearance of my home up. For me to be a felon and have accomplished the things I did was huge. Home ownership wasn't something I took lightly. No, my house wasn't the biggest, baddest or most modern house, but it was mine: all mine.

I checked the mailbox for any mail. My sister lived a few houses down. She normally collected my mail and took it in the house for me, so I wasn't expecting there to be a stockpile of mail setting in there. I took the few magazines and envelopes into the house with me. I sat my keys and mail on the front console table. The house was quiet and vacant of the sweet aromas that accompanied the presence of a woman. I lit a few incense to dull the stale smell of the house. Taking my place on the sofa, I made myself comfortable by turning on the television and allowed ESPN to watch over me as I dozed off.

The loud buzzing and vibrations of my phone alarm woke me from my deep sleep. It was seven in the evening. I had an hour to get ready before picking Evette up. With my freshly groomed hair and beard, it was only fitting that I show up looking like I was feeling like a million bucks. I showered and got dressed. One last look in the floor-length mirror had me feelin' myself. My floral print shirt popped under the blue suit jacket with matching pants and navy Louboutin loafers. I could smell the crisp scent of Creed covering me like a blanket as I hit the evening air. Once in the car, I dialed Evette to let her know I was on my way. I hadn't spoken with her since earlier today. I can't even lie. Her behavior had me feeling some kind of way. I had cut our day short and decided to send her to the spa so that she could clear her mind. I wasn't sure what the fuck was stressing her out, but I was not going to bear the brunt of it. Besides, a little time away from each other might do us some good.

Making my way up US 131 Highway, I reached my exit to Evette's township. Her condo was hidden away in a suburb of Kalamazoo. The predominately white community hosted many of the who's who in business and the professional scene of the city. I hated being out here. The stares from neighbors always provided me with all I needed to know about them. They didn't want my black ass out there just as much as I didn't want to be there. But it was a sacrifice I was willing to endure for love. I entered her condominium complex by keying in the gate code. Within seconds, the white gate lifted, and I drove into the secluded sanctuary.

As I pulled into the parking garage, I immediately noticed that Evette's car was not in the usual spot. I called her cell phone, and it went straight to voicemail. I went inside the house using my key. It looked like Evette had not been there since we first departed earlier this afternoon. The garment bags of clothing I had purchased were still where I placed them. I tried calling her again with the same results. The bags were taken to the bedroom and hung up in the closet. I flipped on the main lights that we generally left on when we headed out for the evening. Checking the time, I decided to meet up with my friends since she was nowhere to be found. I left a note on the table for Evette. I texted the address of the restaurant we were going to and told her to just meet me there if she was feeling up to it. I was a little surprised that she wasn't here. We had discussed going out earlier today. But we had reservations, and I would not keep everyone waiting.

CHAPTER SIX

"Girl, is that him?" Sharmaine asked.
"You already know." Answering her question, I rolled my eyes. I just know he didn't think I was going to jump up and run after him. Nope! Not after that shit he pulled earlier.

"Weren't you supposed to be going out to dinner with him and his friends tonight?" Bridgette chimed in.

"Yeah, but I'm busy right now." I said, knowing damn well I remembered the plans Deshawn and I had. But how was I going to just scurry out of here after I just told Bridgette and Sharmaine what happen earlier today? Deshawn had me all fucked up with the way he was acting. " I'm in no hurry to jump for a man that doesn't know his place. Was the dick hella good, yes. But it wasn't worth the shit he pulled earlier today." I announced. I could see Sharmaine and Bridgette smirk and side eye me.

"So you not going?" Bridgette sarcastically said. Sharmaine just shook her head.

"What I say." I joked as I finished the last of the sweet red California Red wine that was in my stemless glass. Just then, I received the directions to the restaurant from Deshawn. The ladies just looked at me as I placed the phone upside down and engaged in a second round of drinks.

GIVING MY ALL TO YOU

An hour had passed since the first text messages had come through from Deshawn. I guess he wasn't missing my company after all. Bridgette had a late-night date and Sharmaine needed to stop by her mother's house to pick a few things for tomorrow. We decided to call it a night. I thanked them for allowing me to vent my dating woes to them. I dropped them off at their destinations and headed home. Just as I was turning the key to the lock of my condo, another text came through from Deshawn.

> **Deshawn–**
> I hope you're ok. I'm worried. I haven't heard from you. Please call me when you get this message.

I turned on the location finder app on my phone and saw that Deshawn's location had moved to an address that was not the one he had previously sent. I hesitated to text him back. But the liquid courage had kicked in.

> **Me–**
> I'm good. Where are you?

I waited for his reply. He better not lie to me. I already knew the address. It's not like I couldn't just google search the address. Before I succumbed to my insecurities, Deshawn had texted back.

> **Deshawn –**
> We moved the party to the Club 716. A friend of ours is playing in a band here tonight. You should come down and join us.

I didn't respond. I told myself that I was in no shape to pretend that Deshawn had not embarrassed me earlier today. But the wine had me feeling good. I was ready for action and with that, logic had escaped me. I decided to go home and quickly shower and got dressed, putting on the dress Deshawn salivated over that he purchased at the boutique today. I had to admit; I looked damn good. The dress was the right shade of red and graced the curves of my body like it was custom fitted. I put on a pair of gold hoop earrings and my gold bangles. My hair was curly from getting damp in the shower. I sprayed some leave-in conditioner on my coils, rubbed some mango oil through my strands and watched my hair come to life. With a simple makeup look, a cream-colored clutch, and matching trench, I headed out to surprise Deshawn.

I arrived at the club. It was jam packed, and the party had cascaded out in the street as crowds mingled outside to take in their nicotine breaks and engage in small talk. I walked past the smoke and into the busy establishment. I stopped by the bar first and ordered something to calm my already shot nerves. Surveying the scene, I saw Deshawn's friend Eric and his wife, Tamara. The bartender handed me my drink, and I made my way over to the group.

"Hey everyone, sorry for being late. You know me, work never stops." I lied, making light of the real reason I was tardy to the gathering. Deshawn rose from his chair to greet me. He looked damn fine. I smiled as the shocked look on his face met my eyes.

"Hey special lady. I didn't think you were going to make it." He commented as he looked me over and pulled me into him. The smell of his cologne suffocated me as I inhaled him, forgetting everything that happen earlier today. His soft beard brushed against my face as he planted a kiss on my cheek. "You look fucking amazing," he whispered, and I instantly felt my yoni tighten and my sacred juices bubble forth.

"Thank you," I shyly replied.

Deshawn pulled up a chair from a nearby table and welcomed me into the group. I carried on small talk with the ladies at the table as we listened to the band play. Deshawn's eye never left my sight. He stared at me the whole time. His hand rested on the small of my back. His mere presence caused my thighs to tense up with the hope of him getting in between them. I played it cool, although my heart and mind conflicted with each other. I wanted to be mad at him, but the way my body yearned for this man didn't allow me to dwell on the issue from earlier.

The band played a few cover songs. I heard the beat of Uncle Charley's "I Can't Live Without You". My body swayed back and forth. Deshawn caught me in the chair dancing and leaned in and took my hand. He guided me out of my seat and onto the dance floor. At first my attitude was hell naw. But once the beat took over, I gave all the way in. His body pressed against mines as he sang along in perfect pitch. "I Can't live without you girl" sent goosebumps up and down my spine as I rested in his arms. By now the drinks and rhythm got the best of me because we were in a serious tangle. Deshawn could dance and I was no stranger to getting down. The way he twirled me on the floor and then snatched me back into him had me ready to fuck. It was giving big dick energy, and I was here to testify it was all true. "I can't forgive myself if I hurt you, girl," he whispered in my ear.

Deshawn kept me on the dance floor for three more songs. Thank goodness my hair was curly for the evening or it would have sweated out. I was feeling myself. Deshawn was fine as fuck, and I knew that there were a few ladies in there wishing they could be in my shoes. The couple vibes we gave off had his friends egging us on as we smoothly grooved on the dance floor. After the third song, Deshawn took me by the waist and guided me off the floor. We headed over to the bar. There was a quiet spot in the corner. Deshawn ordered drinks for the table. He kissed my hand as we locked eyes.

"Are we good, ma?" he asked.

All I could do was shake my head, yes. He stood behind me as we waited for our drinks. I could feel the impression of his hard pipe trying to penetrate my dress. I slowly grinded on him as the music played. Deshawn gently kissed my neck as we waited for the bartender to finish making the drinks. We were lost in the moment when the bartender laid out the order in front of us. The bartender was cute. She smiled at Deshawn and me and said, "Ok Sis. I see you," I smiled back, thinking; I didn't need her to cosign a damn thing about my man.

We headed back over to the table. I led the way as Deshawn carried the cocktails. The band was on break and the DJ was spinning tunes. I noticed an extra body at the table. When she saw Deshawn and me, she jumped up and walked into Deshawn's now empty arms. Everyone seemed comfortable with her actions expect me.

"Shawn," her soprano voice sang out.

"Vivian," Deshawn replied with the same level of excitement. Their embrace seemed a little too familiar. I stood there, waiting for Deshawn to see my reaction. Playing it as cool as the alcohol would allow me to. I took my glass of wine and took a seat as everyone at the table engaged in the strangers' presence. Then, finally, after ignoring my existence, I heard Deshawn's voice.

"Viv, this is Evette, Evette, this is my dear friend Viv."

Umm, she got a whole ass title, and I was just Evette. I thought to myself as a fake smile blessed our exchanged.

"Oh my goodness, I've heard so much about you," Vivian said as she hugged me.

"Same here." I lied. Deshawn hasn't told me a single thing about this woman. He was too busy toasting up with his boys to notice the darts my eyes were aiming at him. I saw him pull up a chair for Vivian. He planted himself right in between both of us. I watched as the entire group swooned over her. That was when I noticed she was one of the main singers of the band I had just jammed too. I just smiled and listen to the conversations. So far, I knew Vivian was in town for the next few weeks. The band was recording a new album. Which was funny to me because I had never heard of them until tonight. She went on and on about her life and where she was now. I felt like an outsider, especially since Deshawn never mentioned her to me.

I wanted to wipe that silly ass smile off of Deshawn's face, but I was too cute tonight for those antics. The wine, however, had me feeling some kind of way again. We all applauded as the band started up. My hands clapped reluctantly. I watched as Deshawn was all ears and eyes as Vivian took the stage. What really threw me for a loop was what happen next. This bitch dedicated the song she was about to sing to him. There was an awkward quietness that came over the table as everyone except Deshawn looked at me. This negro was too engulfed in the performance to even notice me. At that announcement. I headed to the bar.

"One more glass please," I stated to the male bartender. I was patiently waiting for my glass of wine when two unknown females approached me. One girl whispered loud enough for me to hear her say, I guess he's with her.

"Excuse me," I said, annoyed.

"Your Deshawn's woman, right?" the other girl asked.

I just stared at them with no reply.

" Girl, you better hold on to that," the other girl sated.

"Or what? " The wine urged me to say just as Deshawn approached me.

"Hey Deshawn," the taller girl said as they walked away.

"Baby, you ok?" He asked as I pulled away.

"No, I'm not ok. I am ready to leave." I said, as I headed toward the door.

"Evette, slow down," he said as he grabbed my arm. I looked at him like he better let me go, and he did. "Just wait," he reiterated. I wasn't sure why I did as he stated. Deshawn said his goodbyes to his table of friends as I turned my head to face the exit. I had enough of this night. Hell, I had enough of this entire day. I strolled toward the door and stood in the brisk night's air. I turned around and Deshawn was nowhere in sight. So, I called an Uber. I had an ETA of five minutes. With my coat draped over my shoulders and clutch concealed under my arm, I approached the sidewalk as a car pulled up. The Uber notification appeared on my phone. Tom had arrived in a White Nissan Altima. Right on time, I thought to myself as I turn around and noticed I was still standing by myself. I got in the ride share and instructed Tom to drive away.

CHAPTER SEVEN

"Damn it Evette" I thought to myself as I pulled out of the club parking lot. I told her stubborn ass to wait for me. Immediately, I headed toward her house. The fifteen-minute drive gave me a chance to calm down. This was not the way I wanted this day to end. It started off great, but somewhere between my morning workout and sharing drinks with friends, I fucked up. The sad thing is I had no clue what I did. One thing was for sure, I was 'going to check in with Evette and make sure she got home ok. This shit wasn't cool. Storming away from me like a child was unacceptable behavior. First, she stood me up for our dinner date yesterday and now this. Trying to remain patient with her was a struggle. I'm not sure whether it's work or something else that's stressing her out. I'm bothered by her behavior and her unwillingness to communicate with me what was going on with her. I just know I didn't want my lady wandering around the streets at this time of the night.

I pulled into the parking space in the downtown condominium. The weekend staff was on duty. I waved as I walked past the front desk. I rode the elevator up to the seventh floor. The house was quiet.

"Evette," I called out, with no answer. I walked around the floor plan and noticed Evette's shadow casting its image on the wall. She was sitting in the dark in the front room. I turned the light on.

"I know you heard me call your name. What's up, ma?" I asked as I approached her.

"Deshawn, what do you want?" she dryly answered me with a question.

"What do you mean, what do I want? Why did you leave the club without me? I told you I was coming. How did you get home?" I quizzed her with question after question.

"You don't have the right to ask me anything after the shit you pulled today." Evette said.

"Hold on. You're my woman. I have every right to be concerned about you. Just talk to me, baby." I responded to her statement as I kneeled before her.

"Deshawn, who the fuck is Vivian?" she sternly asked.

"I told you, Viv and I are good friends," I replied, not telling the whole truth. I could tell from her body language that she wasn't buying my half-truth. Her eyes shot bullets through me. I was never one to lie, so I wasn't about to start today. It was just that my relationship with Vivian was complicated. Plus, it was the past. It was something that I also wanted to remain right where it was. I knew Evette wouldn't understand. I didn't hide it from her. It just wasn't worth bringing up. Evette sat there staring at me, mad as hell. I took a deep breath and finally answered her questions again. "Vivian and I used to date back in the day. We were childhood sweethearts. I got locked up, and she went on with her life."

"So, you took me on a date to meet your long-lost love," Evette yelled out and started laughing.

"It's not like that. Viv and I are only friends." I confessed.

"Yea, the type of friend that you talk about your girlfriend and she knows nothing about her. Am I right?," She said as she stood up.

"Our relationship is complicated, but trust me ma, we are just friends. Nothing more." I stated.

"You two seemed real comfortable, a little too comfortable for me." Evette said as she pushed by me. She went over to the bar cart and poured herself another drink.

"Don't you think you had enough to drink for the night? Don't think I didn't notice that you were tipsy when you arrived at the club. Why don't you put that down so that we can talk?" I suggested.

"Negro, I know you are not my father. My daddy been dead for some time now and last I checked; my daddy wasn't no garbage man." She said.

"Ok. I'mma leave. I can see you're not in the right frame of mind to discuss what happened today. I just wanted to make sure that you got home ok. Looks like you're just fine, so I'mma head out." I spoke up after hearing and seeing Evette's reactions.

"What the fuck you mean you about to leave? Where are you going!?" She cried out.

"I'm going to head home. I realize you need some time to yourself." I said shaking my head as I grabbed my keys.

"Fine leave. Go see your Vivian. Bet she'll be excited to see you." Evette slurred her words as she took a sip of her drink.

I just looked at her. "I'll be back tomorrow to check on you," I said as I closed the door behind me.

The button to the elevator doors didn't even turn red. The doors opened, and the car was already waiting. I stepped in and rode the car down to the main floor in silence. I drove home the same way, allowing the night's calmness to ease my headache. It was already two o'clock in the morning. Thoughts of making love to Evette and waking up cuddled next to her had been replaced with her stinging words and toxic behavior. Hopefully tomorrow she will be in a better headspace to discuss her actions.

I climbed into the cold bed. The stillness of the room and the day's events had my mind racing. The only image I wanted to focus on was Evette in that red dress. As mad as she may have been, my baby looked good as fuck. My manhood jumped at the thought of her ass protruding in that dress. I held him in my hand and allowed myself to stroke him as I imagined everything I wanted to do to her tonight. The ringing of my doorbell interrupted my thoughts. I checked my cell phone and the ring camera notification definitely had someone at my door. Thinking it was Evette. I put my sweatpants on without looking at the image. I rushed to the door and opened it. To my surprise, it was Vivian.

CHAPTER EIGHT

"Damn!" I screamed out loud as I recalled everything that happened last night. I was such an ass, I thought as I woke up to an empty bed and a strong hangover. Looking over at the clock I noticed that it was almost noon. I recalled Deshawn stating that he would be over to check on me in the morning. "Oh, shit," I murmured as the realities of last night plagued me. There was no way I wanted him to see me like this. I smelled like stale wine and regret. I had some serious apologizing to do. In my heart, I knew there was nothing going on between him and Vivian. Deshawn truly was the only man that ever only had eyes for me. He never gave me any reason to question his love for me. The way other women looked at him and he ignored them like a plague to stay focused on me. I must be a fool to have said those things to him.

I got up and made a cup of coffee and took two aspirin tablets. Starting the shower, I made sure that my waxed body parts were still smooth. My appointment with the esthetician was later this week and if there was one thing I hated was hair where there shouldn't be. My freshly washed hair hung past my shoulders. I allowed the curls to flow as I cleansed my face. Finding the perfect forgiveness outfit took some time as I tried on outfit after outfit until I finally came across something that would work. A few spritzes of Deshawn's favorite perfume and I was ready to go apologize.

The universe must have been on my side because I made every light on my way to Deshawn's house. Even the traffic on the highway was nonexistent. I pulled up in front of his house. I checked my makeup in the rearview mirror. And pounced out the car in my heels and trench coat. I rang the doorbell and waited for Deshawn to answer. Within minutes, the door opened. Deshawn was wearing a pair of gray sweatpants and no t-shirt. His chiseled abs made the perfect letter v that led you to look at the imprint that formed in his sweatpants. I wasn't sure if it was his morning wood or the chilly midday air that caused him to look swollen, but I was ready either way.

He just stood there. It was unlike him not to be excited to see me. It was weird the way he was acting. "Hi baby. Can we talk?" I hesitantly asked. Knowing that I had said some hurtful things. Deshawn moved aside and allowed me to enter. We didn't spend a lot of time at Deshawn's house. Every time I visited him over here, his decorative style always impressed me. It wasn't the traditional bachelor pad. It had a masculine vibe but was stylish. From the paintings that adorned the walls to the accent pieces on his mantel, everything made sense. The house even smelled good.
"Would you like some coffee? It's not Starbuck's or Bigby's but it's good," He offered.
"Sure. I said as I watched Deshawn fix me a cup of coffee just the way I took it. I stood in the kitchen's doorway and saw the

man who belonged to me. I wasn't sure how to begin to apologize, but I knew I'd better try.

"So talk Evette," he demanded.

"Well,.. I just wanna apologize. I didn't mean the things I said to you yesterday. I should have never said that to you. I don't know what's come over me. Baby, I'm so sorry for the way I treated you." I said as I untied my colored trench coat. Once the coat opened, I allowed it to fall off my shoulders, exposing my voluptuous figure that was covered in the lingerie set that Deshawn picked out just twenty-four hours ago. The hot pink and black number cuffed my 38DD's just right and the heart cutout covered just enough of my valley to be intriguing. The string in the back had a bow on the top that sat at the crack of my full round ass as the rest hid between my cheeks.

I saw the look on Deshawn's face. It wasn't at all what I was expecting. He didn't have a comment. In fact, he walked away, leaving me standing there half naked. I didn't know what to think. I'd just apologized, and this man was acting like he didn't hear me or see me. He walked back into the kitchen with a t-shirt and tossed it at me.

"You might want to put this own." He said as he took a sip of his coffee. Just then, I heard the front door open.

"Shawn, I got breakfast! " The familiar voice called out.

I turned to see Vivian carrying two bags of takeout. I could tell from the look on her face that she wasn't expecting me, nor was I expecting to see her.

"Well, it's a good thing I brought enough to feed an army," she joked as she stared at me.

"Vivian and I were getting ready to have brunch. You should join us," Deshawn said. He picked up my coat off the kitchen floor and took it to his bedroom.

"I'm sorry. Should I leave you two alone to talk?" Vivian asked.

"No, don't be silly. You just said there was enough for all of us," Deshawn stated, grinning at me.

I was hot as hell. But I kept my cool. "Evette, you might want to go get changed."

My gaze fell on Vivian and Deshawn before I headed to the bathroom suite in Deshawn's bedroom. I put the t-shirt on that he gave me. I was fuming. This nigga had me fucked up. I came over here to apologize, and his ex- girlfriend shows up with food. Like this shit wasn't planned. No wonder he didn't show up bright and early at my place. I took a deep breath. My mind was racing a million thoughts per minute, so I needed to collect my thoughts. I wasn't sure what was going on and before I go back in there and act a fool, it was best I calm down and allow this to play out.

I walked back into the kitchen wearing the t-shirt Deshawn gave me. Deshawn was busy fixing plates, and Vivian was sitting at the table. The small banter between them stopped as I approached.

"Evette, we have eggs, waffles, pancakes, home fries and grits. What would you like?" Deshawn asked.

I watched as he handed Vivian her plate. There was no way this skinny bitch was going to eat all of that food, I thought to myself.

"I'll just have some eggs, grits and home fries," I uttered, feeling defeated. I didn't think I could do this. It was too much. I just wanted to apologize, not have fucking breakfast with his long-lost girlfriend. I felt the tears approaching, and quickly hid them behind my boss bitch attitude. Deshawn handed me my plate as he sat down at the head of the table. He didn't even think about sitting next to me.

"So, last night, Vivian and I caught up." Deshawn said as he looked at me. I felt a burning sensation creep up within my core as I looked at Deshawn.

" Yes, my husband insisted I wake him up and have Shawn come out to hang with us," Vivian stated.

"Husband" I asked, surprised.

"Yes, my husband is the drummer in the band. You two left so early last night, you didn't get a chance to meet him." Vivian confessed.

"Where is he at now?" I asked. "He's at the studio. Business meeting." Vivian replied. I had to admit this conversation wasn't what I was expecting to hear. Instantly my blood pressure decreased and thoughts of what if all went away. I looked at Deshawn as his vacant stare began to warm up.

I listened as Vivian talked about her life as a singer and married life on the road. Hearing her talk about her life and the past connection with Deshawn, I could see why they were still friends. I wasn't jealous of her anymore. I was more ashamed of my behavior.

We finished up eating and Vivian stated she needed to get to the studio.. Before she left, she asked to speak with me. I followed her into the front room as Deshawn rinsed the dishes and prepared a load for the dishwasher.

"What's up, Vivian?" I asked.

"Don't you hurt him," she stated, just as bold and bad as she could.

"I have no intention of hurting Deshawn. His heart is in excellent hands," I insisted, taking a defensive stand.

"It didn't look that way last night." She confided.

"I don't know what you think you know, but Deshawn and I are good." I replied.

"He loves you." Vivian commented.

"I know that. And as long as you know, all is good," I stated.

Deshawn walked into the front room. "Y'all not talking about me, are you? " He laughed.

"You wish," Vivian laughed as she looked at me. It was at that moment I knew she not just loved Deshawn but was still in love with him. She wasn't expecting me to show up. Lord knows what she might have tried if I didn't. Vivian wasn't just being a good friend. She still held a torch for Deshawn. But as I was looking at her, he was watching me. I didn't even allow that revelation to bother me.

Vivian noticed Deshawn staring at me as well.

"Alright, you two. I'm going to leave you alone. Evette, it was a pleasure meeting you finally. Please take care of our guy." She slyly said as she hugged me goodbye and gave Deshawn a kiss on the cheek.

"I'll take real good care of my man," I said as she left out the front door and looked back at the two of us in the doorway. I waved as Deshawn closed the door. He didn't even wait to see her drive off. Something I knew he would do for me. She was his past, and I was his now. There was no need for me to worry about Viv. If there was, I wouldn't still be standing in his t-shirt in his house.

I walked back toward Deshawn's bedroom and grabbed my coat. I took off his t-shirt and placed it on the bed. I put my coat on and headed toward the door. I walked back into the front room. Deshawn was sitting on the sofa, naked. His erect penis stood at attention and was the only thing I saw.

"You leaving? I thought you came over to apologize." He said, grinning.

"I thought you.. " I attempted to answer before interrupting me.

"Take the coat off." He commanded. He held his thick, long dick in his hands. My coat fell to the wood floor. "Turn around," his voice whispered. I did as instructed. Deshawn's eyes roamed over my body as I watched him stroke his stick. My body slowly moved as he rubbed himself. As if music was playing in the background, seductively my body gyrated to the rhythm of his hand moving up and down his shaft. The way his fingers cuffed the tip of his dick turned me on. My mouth watered as I spun around and dropped it low. Deshawn's intense eyes told me he wanted me just as bad as I wanted him.

I crawled over to him on all fours, placing myself between his muscular legs. Without saying a word, I took all of him in. I coaxed his swollen stick down my throat without gagging, past my tonsils as my tongue massaged him. Deshawn sat there and allowed me to have my way with him. I sucked on him, creating streams of saliva, covering his dick as I stroked and bobbed on his member. The way I spit on it and moaned and squealed caused him to explode deep in my throat. I drank every drop of his hot liquid as he headed my damp hair by the handfuls. My steady head movements continued until I felt him come alive again. His dick jerked with a vengeance inside the warmth of my mouth. Deshawn grabbed me up and pulled me onto him. The way his tongue tasted his seed as his deep kiss smothered me, turned me on. My pussy was wet with anticipation of swallowing him deep inside my walls. As he entered me, I whispered "I'm sorry".

"Baby, I already know," Deshawn said, moaning loudly and biting his lip. "I know, baby, and I forgive you. Now take this dick and let me love you." He said as I held on tight and enjoyed the ride.

CHAPTER NINE

By the middle of the work week, I was already feeling drained. We had one more street to clear before lunch time. The fellas and I opted to stop by this sandwich shop that just opened up off of Burdick. We heard good things about the food and decided to show them some support. Mike drove the truck while Greg and I held on to the back of the truck as we coasted into the extra parking space for the sandwich shop. I immediately walked over to the outside hose and rinsed off my hands. My pocket size soap and hand sanitizer always came in handy for days like this. Working for the sanitation department was not for the weak. You can learn a lot about people and their trash. One thing all three of us could agree on was that as a whole people were nasty. And for seventy, maybe eighty hours a week, I saw firsthand what that looked and smelled like.

Me and the guys rinsed off the griminess of the early morning haul. I took my jumpsuit off and rested it on the hood of the truck and the fellas followed suit. We entered the eatery just as the lunch rush started. The line formed quickly as people of all walks of life came in to order their food. Everything on the menu looked good. I asked the guy that took our order what he recommended. I always felt when in doubt ask the employee.

And if the employee didn't eat at the place they worked, that was a sign that I should rethink my takeout options. All three of us went with the recommended special that was backed by the employee and the guy behind us in line.

Within minutes, our order was ready. So far, the customer service and speediness of the deli was good. The only thing left was to try was the food. We took our bags and headed outside. There were a few picnic benches in the back of the standalone building. We copped a seat and dug in. From the silence and the way we were all focused on what was in front of us, one would reach the conclusion that the food was good. After a few bites, Mike broke the silence.

"So when you gonna introduce me to that fine ass friend of Evette's."

I laughed, "Who Bridgette?"

"Yeah man, girl is bad," Mike smiled as he finished the bite of his sandwich.

"Man, you better leave that alone." I warned, as I chuckled.

"Why you hatin?'. Greg said as he dapped Mike up.

"Listen, I told y'all Evette's friends are a different breed. I'm not saying you not good enough, but I'm saying you ain't ready for that, my boy." I clearly stated as I walked away to throw my trash out.

"What I hear is that you don't think I'm good enough. Shit, I dated women I knew were too damn good for me. It elevated my stock. When we broke up, I was getting pussy left and right." Mike joked.

"I know that's right, Big Mike," Greg cheered.

"Fellas, I don't think you're listening. I think you're too good for them. Them chicks are something else." I shook my head as I patted Mike on the shoulders.

"Man, come on," Greg said as we started to walk back to the truck.

"Naw seriously. Don't do it. But if you insist, I'll pass the word on," I said. Mike smiled.

"That's what I'm talking about," Mike said.

"Yeah, you say that now. Don't come to me when this shit backfires on you. I tried to warn your thirty ass." I laughed as we suited back up and took our positions on the truck.

We pulled out of the parking lot and headed back into the city to clear a few more streets of their trash pickup.

I cooked blackened honey salmon with Brussel sprouts and yellow spiced rice. Just as I was done cooking. Evette walked through the front door. Ever since our last fall out, she has been spending time at my place, which was a pleasant change of pace. Seeing her always brought a smile to my face.

"Hey pretty lady," I said as she walked in and planted a tender kiss on my cheek.

"Hey boo. It smells so good in here." She complimented me and my culinary skills.

"Here, take a seat and let me feed you. Removing her coat, I kneeled down to unbuckle her t-strap peep toe heels. I loved taking care of Evette. The image of my mother working hard and my father's loving attention to her before his unexpected passing is etched in my mind. I think my mother searched the rest of her days for his replacement and came up empty. Their relationship showed me so many things in such a short period of time. The way he loved my mother had me believing in love everlasting. My father, without say a word, taught me how to love a woman. And I promised myself the next time I gave my heart to someone, I would show that special someone just how real love looked.

Evette ate every bit of food on her plate as did I. Evette cleared the dishes and what little food that was left she packaged up and set in the refrigerator. While she was doing that, I went into the bathroom and ran the water in the tub. I added a few bath bombs I had picked up for Evette since she had spent time over here. I got undressed and allowed my body to sink into the heated porcelain lounge.

The room was dimly lit, and I had candles going. Evette joined me as soon as she was done with the kitchen. I watched as she peeled the day's layers off her beautiful melanated skin. I gazed over her stretch marks that my tongue had traveled and knew so well. Each one told the story of her strength, her journey, and the pain she had witnessed. Her full hips screamed motherhood as they gave way to her perfectly bodacious backside. Every feature on Evette's body was masterfully sculpted. It was portioned as if God knew one day I would be right here admiring his work. She smiled at me as I extended my hand to assist her with stepping into the tub.

The steam eased her tensed body into mine as she sat between my legs. We sat there and allowed the stillness of the room to free us from the outside world. Evette's soft body rested on me as the steam from the scolding water moved slowly between us. My fingers danced on her arms and across her clavicle bone as we lay immersed in the room's darkness. The scent of the bath bombs and candles set the tone for relaxation. We moved in silence like mimes, washing each other up with our soapy washcloths. Evette was gentle as she ran the soap across my body. I returned the favor as my hands slid over her breasts and down the front of her body. We caressed each other until the body wash had covered us. We rinsed off by holding each other close and allowing the tub of water to drench us.

I dried Evette off, admiring her grown ass womanly features. Without warning, I picked her up. I heard her squeal from the surprise gesture.

"Put me down," she whispered.

"When I'm ready," I whispered, looking into her eyes.

"Why do you do that?," She questioned.

"Do what? Show you how I feel?" I replied. Her silence told me she was rethinking her initial question. I sat her on the bed. She shied away from looking at me.

"Look at me E." I softly commanded. Her eyes rose to meet mine. Then I continued, " I'm not sure of the kind of men you fucked with in your past. But I'm not them. If I wanna choose you, I will. If I want to show you how much I love you, I'll do it. If I feel like shouting to the world that you're my woman, I'll do it. I need you to stop trying to prevent me from being the man that you deserve. Can you do that?" I asked.

She was quiet. I didn't stop staring at her. I saw her try to look away. And that's when I saw the tears flow freely down her face. I kneeled so that I could make sure she saw and heard me as I wiped her face dry. "Evette. Don't do that."

"Do what?" she whispered.

"Tell yourself you don't deserve this. Because you do. You deserve to be loved, worshipped, and cared for. We all do." I stated, lifting her chin up so she could see me.

"But how could you love me? I'm not the.." she said before I interrupted what I knew she was about to say.

"E, baby. You are the finest woman in the room. There isn't a woman alive that can compare to what I see in you. You're my perfect package. Don't you know that?" I asked.

She hesitated. "But I look at Vivian and the other women I see fighting for your attention and then I see me. I look nothing like them.

"E, there is a reason Vivian is my past. She cheated on me. I could never forgive her for that. I know she regrets it to this day. She and I could never be more than friends. As far as other women are concerned, I'm not. As long as you're on my arm, that's all I need."

"But I'll never be skinny like.."

"Stop that. I love you for you. If I wanted that type of woman, I'll have her. You think I didn't know you had curves? Hell, that's why I took a second look at you. Your smile was the reason I pressed up on you again that night at the club. All night long, I was shooting shots. I don't work that hard at work, but I saw you were worth it. I knew you had stretch marks. Every inch of your beautiful body, I'm going to explore with my lips. Don't you see how much I love you, girl." I proclaimed.

Her eyes lit up with me, saying the words everyone wants to hear. "You do?" she questioned.

"E, if you don't see, it's because you're too caught up on what everyone thinks. I would go to the end of time, move heaven and hell for you. You're the woman for me, baby. I backed up and headed to my dresser, opening the first drawer. I pulled out a small blue velvet box. Bending down on one knee. This wasn't how I had planned it, but under the circumstances, it seemed appropriate.

"Evette Monae Watts, I love you more than anything. You are my first thought in the morning and my last thought before I sleep. I could never forgive myself if I let you go. I can't live without you and I think it's time I make this official. Will you do me the honor of being my wife and allow me to love you until we are no more."

The steady stream of tears that rolled down Evette's face and the permanent smile that etched itself on her face told me her answer, but I needed to hear it, anyway. And then she spoke the words I longed to hear.

"Yes, Yes. I'll marry you! She shouted with joy.

I reached in and kissed her full lips. I took the ring out of the box and slid the ring on the appropriate finger. The half cart pear shaped ring shined bright on her manicured hand. We kissed again and again. Hopefully now Evette knew my intentions with her heart had always been pure. I wasn't just playing the role; I was playing to win. And considering where I came from and what she had been through, I needed both of us to win at this love game.

CHAPTER TEN

I was so excited! Today, me and my girls are headed to Chicago to do some dress shopping. I have been on a high ever since Deshawn proposed. He really loved me and I loved me some him. It was me, Sharmaine, Bridgette, Carmen, and CeCe. I had asked them all to be my bridesmaids, and they surprised me by accepting my request. I was more surprised that Sharmaine and Bridgette agreed to stand up for me, considering they both had been Deshawn's biggest critics. Would it have hurt me if they didn't want to be at the wedding? Well, yes, but they were willing to put aside their dislike of him for my happiness. I was glad that they were on board. Besides, who the hell else would I ask to be my bridesmaids?

I planned a girls' weekend full of fun while visiting the windy city. First was dress shopping. I had two appointments while in town. I figured if I didn't find my dress at one shop, then I had another bridal boutique lined up just in case. Either way, I wasn't leaving Chicago without my dress. There was nothing in Michigan for me. I wouldn't be caught dead in one of those basic ass bridal dresses. I had been to enough weddings in Michigan where the bride wore a dress I had seen once, maybe even twice, on someone else. My fashion sense and lifestyle would never allow me to comply with the basic bitch syndrome that most brides conformed to in Michigan. I needed something as unique as I was. A dress that showed off my curves and, above all, made me feel like I was the most beautiful woman in the room.

After dress shopping, we were going to lunch, followed by some shopping. I planned a late dinner at Luella's Southern Kitchen. I was not leaving Chicago without eating some of her famous biscuits. If the ladies aren't worn out from all the shopping, maybe we could hit the town before we head back to the hotel. But for now, I needed to hunt down my dress, and trying on dresses after eating was a no-no. That protein drink I had was going to be put to the test today. The container said that it suppresses your appetite for up to five hours. Today, I was going to test out their claim. I couldn't take the chance of being bloated or feeling sluggish. No, today had to be perfect. Besides, it was already stressful enough to be searching for a wedding dress that would fit my curves the way I had envisioned.

The Uber pulled up in front of the Bridal Boutique located in Orland Park. We exited the XL Uber and cheered as we entered the storefront. The boutique was adorable. They dressed the windows up with mannequins wearing various styles of wedding dresses. The up-lighting created a romantic feeling as the details of the dresses danced in the windows. I was in awe. I had never thought this day would come. It wasn't my first time in a bridal store. It was just the first time I was the bride. I had been the forever bridesmaid. I had a closet full of colorful dresses outlining the last fifteen years of weddings. From sorority sisters, cousins, and best friends, I had stood up for a dozen brides and now it was finally my turn.

Within minutes, the slender old lady greeted us.

"You must be the bride- Ms. Evette Watts," she spoke, extending her hand to me.

"What gave me away?" I asked with a smile.

"I can spot a bride to be from a mile away. Plus, I do my homework. How is your stay in Chicago so far?," she asked.

"Just fine," I stated.

"And you found the boutique ok?" she continued.

"Yes, thank you." I replied.

"That's good to hear. This must be your bridesmaids. Hello ladies. If you can all follow me. You'll be trying on dresses in our Victorian room. My name is Glynis. Your consultant today will be Natasha. She will be right with you." Glynis stated as she guided us to our room.

As we walked through the storefront, the excitement and chatter of brides to be filled the air. There were racks and racks of breathtaking, exquisite and glamourous gowns. A girl could become overwhelmed sifting through the sea of lace and satin. Luckily for me, I knew exactly which dresses I wanted to try on. I also made sure that the dress came in my size. The horror stories of curvy brides and finding the right dress led me to seek out boutiques and designers that catered to my style and my physique. It was the main reason I chose this particular bridal shop. A popular bridal magazine listed them in their top ten boutiques in a feature showcasing designers for plus size brides. I immediately fell in love with one designer's style and knew I had to try on his unique creations.

Natasha greeted us with champagne and an assorted array of cheese and a fruit platter. Before getting started, she and I sat away from the group for my private consultation. I shared with her the dresses from the magazine that wanted to try on. Natasha agreed to pull those items for me. I also gave her some leeway to pull a few dresses she thought would look great on me. And with a blink of an eye, Natasha was off and running. I returned to my gang of bridesmaids as they roamed the aisles of bridesmaids' gowns to try on. We all agreed that black was the bridesmaid's dress color. They could wear whatever design they chose, it just needed to be from the same designer and black.

By the time Natasha came back, her hands were full of flowing dresses that were hung on satin covered hangers. She escorted me into the private dressing room to get started with trying dresses on. Before my appointment, I had been instructed to come wearing the undergarments that I would more than likely be wearing on my wedding day. So, I did just that. My shapewear and strapless bra made the fitting of the dress come to life. My curves looked banging in the first dress I tried on. Natasha laced me up in the corset style mermaid dress as I stared at myself in the full-length mirror. I looked stunning. We didn't start with my first-choice dress, but one that Natasha had chosen. Our strategy was to warm up the critics who were known to be vocal, then gradually present them with my top picks.

But as I looked at myself in the mirror in this dress, the more I thought it would be hard to beat this dress. Natasha helped me gather up the bottom of the dress as she ushered me out of the fitting room. I stood on the pedestal as my friends had a 360-

degree view of my fabulousness. At first, the group was silent. I heard gasps as I entered the viewing area. You would have thought that I came out naked. But the silence soon turned to excitement as they applauded my first selection. It could have been because it was the first dress, but everyone loved it; at first.

I was hella confident in the dress I was wearing. I remember just minutes before I admired my shapely physique in the mirror. The way the corset bodice snatched me in had me looking like a BBL model. Sharmaine broke her silence and asked how I felt in the dress. It was something in her tone that had me questioning everything I knew to be true. Bridgette soon joined in.
"That ain't it!" she smacked her lips and took a sip of champagne.
Natasha asked me how I felt in the dress. And to my surprise, I humbled myself and agreed that this dress wasn't it. The look on Natasha's face was shocking. She was sure we were on the right path, considering our conversation moments earlier. Back to the dressing room, I went. Natasha helped me out of the dress and we were on to the next dress. This went on for the reminder of the appointment. I would try on a dress and Sharmaine or Bridgett would have something negative to say about it or me in it. I was feeling defeated. By the time we got to the dress I had dreamed of wearing, I didn't even have the heart to try it on. Natasha suggested I put the dress on and not show my friends. I agreed. And even though Natasha and I agreed I looked amazing in the dress; they had crushed my spirit and I was in no mood to pick out my dress.

Natasha had me rate the dresses from one to ten. She wrote my top five choices on a card. When I was ready, I could return to the boutique and make my final decision. I agreed. She finished up taking the measurements and fitting for the bridesmaids' dresses. They all made their deposits for their gowns while I left empty-handed. I canceled the next appointment. There was no way I wanted to torture myself again by trying on dresses and walking away without making a decision. I was done and just wanted to go back to the hotel.

The ladies and I made plans to go out later that evening. After arriving back at the hotel, I took a much-needed nap. Forgoing lunch and shopping with my bridesmaids, I couldn't shake my disappointment at wedding gown shopping. Who knew that this process would be so stressful? Maybe I just needed to sleep on it. I had the dress information and my body measurements that were written on the card Natasha gave me. Hopefully, in the morning I could think clearly and make my decision without the help of my friends. After all, I really did like the first dress I tried on.

I woke up and checked the time. It was seven-sixteen in the evening. I slept for a good four hours. Me and my clique had dinner reservations at eight-thirty. I had almost an hour to get ready. I showered and reapplied a fresh make-up look. We were also going out on the town after dinner. I was looking cute in my faux leather Gucci dress. My hair was set in wavy curls as it cascaded down my back. Slipping on my heels before taking one last glance in the mirror, I was ready.

I arrived down in the hotel's lobby to see CeCe and Carmen patiently waiting for my arrival.

"Hey sleepy head," Carmen joked.

"We missed you at brunch," CeCe commented.

"I'm so sorry, ladies. That whole trying on bridal dresses took all the energy I had." I lamented.

"That and Sharmaine's hating ass," Carmen slyly joked.

"Oh, come on, ladies. She is just looking out. Besides, she was right." I said, not convincing anyone but myself.

"If that's what you want to call it." CeCe smirked.

"Just remember, those two are your friends. But if I were you, I'd watch my back. They both looked mighty green," Carmen stated.

We were finishing up our conversation just as Sharmaine and Bridgett approached.

"What y'all heifas talking about?" Bridgett asked.

"Just you and Bridgette and how much fun we had this afternoon shopping." Carmen jumped in, teasing as she gave me the side eye.

"I know that's right; we had a ball. Plus, I coped some serious looks that I know no one in Michigan will be wearing. The next time we hit them streets, all eyes will be on me," Sharmaine bragged as CeCe and Carmen looked on in disgust. I knew these ladies were like oil and vinegar. But for the sake of my wedding, they all agreed to get along.

"Where is Sharmaine?" I asked, breaking the tension.

"She's on her way down. She took a last-minute call." Sharmaine stated as she took a seat on the couch in the lobby and took her selfies.

I quickly texted Sharmain that our ride would be here soon and to head downstairs. She hit me back with the thumbs up emoji.

We had dinner at Goosefoot. The meal was a complete experience and well worth the two hundred dollars per person price for the chef's table. The way we all were taking pictures of our food had us looking like foodies. With each course, the food got more and more intriguing. It looked almost too good to eat. The avant-garde modern twist to the menu won all of us over. Goosefoot was sophisticated and bright, as was the food. And for once on this trip, we were all in agreement.

The night was not over. Sharmaine heard about this bar that played nineties old school Hip Hop and R&B. So, after dinner, we headed there to finish our trip to Chicago. We pulled up to the bar. Our ride share driver let us out and you could hear the bass from the music playing all the way outside. There was a small cover charge to enter, which we gladly paid. The crowd was jammin' to the tunes the DJ was spinning. We walked through and found a booth that we could all sit at. As soon as we got comfortable, a hostess came over to our table and took our drink orders. We must have come at the right time because within minutes, the bar became crowded with people already to get their groove on. Our hostess brought over our libations and a menu. We could order a hookah station along with finger foods. We were all full from dinner but agreed to partake in a hookah session.

The music was giving serious throwback nostalgic vibes. Me, Carmen and CeCe headed to the Dance floor as soon as we heard the beat to MJB's Real Love. Every female on the dance floor was singing their hearts out as the song played. The DJ cut in the song by mixing in Nas–"If I Ruled the World" and before long Brandy's "Baby, Baby, Baby " was echoing through the speakers. The DJ had us all in our feelings as song after song we stayed on the dance floor. I was getting ready to head back to the table when a strange hand tapped me on the shoulder. I turned around to see who it was. Never in a million years did I expect it to be Radir Huff. Until that moment, I had forgotten that he moved to Chicago. I hadn't seen I'm in almost eight years. It took me five years to get this man out of my system, and here he was.

"Hey beautiful," he leaned in and whispered to me. The DJ had switched up the musical selection and was now playing old school reggae. Before I could even say anything or better yet walk away, Radir had grabbed my hand and, like a bad after-school special, I followed his lead on the dance floor. The beat of Chaka Demus and Pliers brought our bodies closer than they should have been as our bodies collided from our rocking back and forth. I slowly turned around to serve him my ass to grind on as the slow wine of my hips kept up with his steady sway. Damn, this nigga was everything I didn't need right now. He looked even better than I recalled. We dipped it low and I could feel the impression of his erection pressed against my ass. I should have left. Instead, I allowed my body to fold into his as Buju Banton rang out over the crowd.

After the third song, and several dutty wines with the man who literally caused my soul to have a chain reaction, I caught my breath and sense. I thanked him for the dance and, as gracefully as I could, walked away from our grinding session. Internally, I smiled. My outside appearance stays on resting bitch face. There was no way Radir nor the girls at the table were going to know anything else.

"BITCH! Don't act like we didn't just see that!," CeCe blurted out loud.

" Where did the devil come from?" Sharmaine sarcastically. She rolled her eyes, and I saw it. I knew all too well how everyone felt about Radir.

"I do not know. He tapped me on my shoulder and next thing I knew we were dancing." I said as I took a sip of my drink, hoping that there were no more questions.

"Do we need to remind you about what he did to you?" Carmen stated.

"No, you don't. I'm not stunting Radir. He said hi, we danced, and that was all there was to it. I'm fuck nigga free and would prefer to stay that way." I commented.

"Girl, I know that's right," CeCe chimed in.

"Well, I wouldn't say all that, but we certainly will not be doing Mr. Huff's bullshit again." Bridgett said as she gave me the side eye.

"Listen here. We didn't come here for Radir to dampen the mood. I'mma suggest that yall get your asses on that dance floor once. Ain't no man gonna be coming over to this table with all yall cackling hens. Get out there and shake some ass!" I joked as a few of the ladies took their drinks and marched to the center of the dance floor to do just as I had instructed. The DJ had just finished playing some house music. I needed to catch my breath. It wasn't the dancing that had me stunned. Radir was like a bad omen. Something my heart and pussy swore off eight years ago. And the way I easily gave into him on the dance floor scared the shit out of me.

CHAPTER ELEVEN

"**M**an, so you really going through with it?" Rell jokingly asked.

"Yea, man. She's the one." I proudly said, as a grin came across my face.

"The player is hanging up his jersey after all this time. I never thought I would live to see the day." Mike sarcastically said.

"But on some real shit, I'm happy for you bruh," Greg said as we dapped up.

"Thanks, G. It's time. Plus, I can't see myself living without E. I mean she's the complete package." I stated.

"Shidd, ain't nothing else out here yo. I damn near broke my dick messing around with this young chick. She steady screaming go deeper. My stupid ass gone try and fucked around and slipped out and tried to ram her. I said never again. My ass next. You watch and see. Imma be walking down the aisle next year." Calvin clowned as we all laughed at his story. "Yall think I'm playing. Imma find me a oh Johnny girl like Ray!" he continued.

We all burst out laughing. "Yo Bro, you crazy," Mike laughed out loud.

"All I'm saying is I'm too old for this shit. I shouldn't be sweating like I played a game of pickup after sex. I feel like I be battle dancing these hoes." Calvin laughed.

"That's because you be fucking them twentysomethings." I joked.

"Yeah, what you need to do is make love. Leave that fucking shit to them youngins." Eric stated.

"See Eric talking that mature shit. But not everyone can find a wife as fine as yours. No offense." Rell stated.

"None taken. All y'all got to do is stop playing these little boy games and man the fuck up. Once you do that, all the fine real women will find you." Eric stated.

"You said that like it's a new cologne and shit," Mike joked.

"Nigga, it's called swag and as long as your ass out here eaten bootie and leaving in the middle of the night, then your tires will continue to get slashed." Eric laughed, and we all joined in.

" I remember that! Ol' girl got mad that you put it on her and wouldn't return her calls." Rell chimed in.

"Yea, cause that fool ate the bootie!" I laughed.

"That was the funniest voice message I had ever heard." Greg stated.

"And y'all wonder why I don't want to be out here in these streets no mo." I laughed harder.

"Just promise us you're not going to be one of those husbands that dip on their friends," Mike stated. The room got quiet. I could tell the fellas had concerns, but they had no reason to be alarmed.

"Fellas, I'll be the nigga that stands before you now. The only thing that is changing is Evette will be my wife. She comes before all you niggas, and rightfully so. I'm fucking her and she'll have my last name. Other than that, I'm the same." I spoke up.

"We will see," Mike said.

"Naw, nigga, we won't. Imma still hang with the fellas and Imma be with my wife. And on the off chance y'all get right, we might even co-mingle. But ain't no change up happening with me." I stated firmly.

I could tell from the eye glances a few believed me and a few of the fellas would let time verify my words. It was all good with me. Truth be told, the only person I needed to prove myself to was me. My decision to get married was mine to make. They would just have to respect it, just like I respected their right to do whatever they wanted to do with their lives.

After the fellas left, I was ready to call it a night. Just then, the phone rang. I looked at the time and it was one in the morning. Who the fuck could this be? Evette was in Chicago with her girls and wasn't due back until tomorrow afternoon. I answered, thinking it could be an emergency, being that it was from an unknown number.

"Yo." I said calmly.

"Shawn, it's me," Vivian's small voice cried out.

"Viv, what's wrong?" I asked, now sitting up in the bed.

"Can I come over?" she asked.

"Yeah. You need me to come get you?" I asked, alarmed at the tone of her voice. I could tell she was crying.

"No, I'll be there in ten minutes," Vivian said before hanging up the phone.

I quickly got up. My gray sweatpants and a tank top were the easiest clothing items to throw on. I started cleaning up the remaining beer bottles and glassware that were left over from the night's card game. I lit a candle to freshen the air. Vivian was at the door in ten minutes flat as the Ring camera notified me that she was here. I walked to the front of the house and let Vivian in.

I could tell that she had been crying, just as I suspected. She walked in and took a seat on the couch. She kicked off her heels and cuddled up on the couch with the chenille throw that was draped over the arm of the sofa.
"Can I get you something?" I asked, breaking the silence.
"Yes, a bottle of gin," she replied.
"Oh shit. It's like that, Viv. Ok. I got you. After realizing we had emptied the gin, I walked back to the kitchen and grabbed two glasses and a bottle of Tito's. I headed back over to the sofa and sat down beside her, "We talkin or drinking?" I asked.
"Just pour," she stated.
I obliged. The room was full of silence and the smell of a sandalwood candle from Bath and Body Works. I watched as she took down shot after shot. We sat in silence for thirty minutes. I wasn't sure what was going on with Vivian, but all that drinking and I wasn't sure if she had eaten anything. It could only lead to a night of her hugging my toilet because, if memory serves me right, she wasn't that big of a drinker. I slid off the couch and made my way back to the kitchen. I grabbed a few things out of the fridge and made my famous grilled cheese sandwich. It wasn't a lot, but at least it was something that would soak up some of that alcohol.

Vivian devoured that sandwich. Her tear-stained face showed her anguish. And although I wasn't sure what was going on, I was glad I could be here for her. But I had questions. Like where was her husband and why was he not comforting her? I figured that Vivian just needed to gather her thoughts and emotions. I would hear about what happened now or later. My concern now was making sure Vivian was ok. We sat there in the living room in silence. I occasionally caught Vivian watching me. Slowly, she opened up.

"Shawn, remember when we were together? How is everything used to be so simple?" she asked.

"Yeah. We didn't have all the stress, responsibility, and experience we have today. Shid, if I knew what I know now, things would be different." I replied.

"Like you and me?" Vivian hesitantly added.

"What about you and me?" I quizzed. There was an awkward pause before Vivian's eyes met mine. "What's going on Viv? Why are you here?"

"Shawn... I.. I still love you." She confessed.

Her truthful statement took me aback. I didn't know what to say. I assumed that when I got locked up that she moved on. At first, she would come to visit every week. Hell, even several times a week. She kept my commissary full and the care packages coming. Vivian wrote to me and even answered all my calls. I thought she was willing to do the bid with me, which was something I told her she didn't need to do. I was a big boy and knew the consequences of the lifestyle I lived. Asking her to stop living her life for me is something I could never do. So I didn't trip when the calls stopped and the visits became less until eventually it all ceased.

"Shawn, say something," she whispered.

"What do you want me to say?" I asked.

"Say you love me, too. Say you want me the way I want you." She stated.

"Viv, you're married. You have a family. What we had was..." Vivian interrupted me.

"What we had was real." She stated.

"It couldn't have been that real." I said, frustrated. My hands washed over my face, wondering why now. Why would she pull this shit? It took me ten years to get her out of my system. I waited and waited for a letter, for her to answer my calls or to come visit me until I had to finally given up. I used to eat and sleep, thinking about Vivian. She used to be my everything. She was the only girl that understood me. It wasn't about the stacks of money, the power I possessed; she never attempted to change me. Vivian was supposed to be my ride or die. Her love made it easy for me to have hope, considering all the shit I had done.

"But it was," Vivian tried to reassure me.

"Vivian, I am not doing this with you. Not now. If you want to stay here tonight, the guest room is all yours. But this conversation is dead." I warned.

"But Shawn..." she attempted to argue.

"No, but's. It's late. You're drunk and I'm tired." I yelled out. My baritone voice echoed through the house, startling Vivian. The conversation was over for me. I walked over to the alarm pad to make sure I had set the security alarm. I then walked toward my room and closed the door behind me. All I could remember was the scared looked on Vivian's face as I drifted off to sleep.

By the time I woke, Vivian had left. She was one of only three people who had full access to my home. So, it was no surprise that I didn't hear the alarm go off when she left. I got rid of the empty liquor bottle and glassware from the front of the house. I straighten up the living room and did the same to the guest room.

Viv had left her earrings on the nightstand. I picked them up and took them to my bedroom and placed them on my dresser, still thinking about last night and the bomb that Viv dropped on me. I desperately needed to blow off some steam. I grabbed my gym bag and water bottle, quickly got dressed, and headed to the gym.

I was deep into my core exercises before a young lady interrupted me. I had my earbuds in with the music playing and barely heard anything she said.

"Excuse me," I said, taking out my left earbud.

"I'm sorry" she said. "I didn't see that you had that in your ears. Is that your Black truck out front? The guy at the front desk said that it might be your car. Your alarm is going off." She stated as she walked away to continue her exercise routine. I stopped what I was doing and made my way to the front of the gym. From the inside vestibule, I could tell that something was off with the image of my truck. It wasn't until I walked up to the vehicle that I could clearly see that my rear tire was flat. Upon further inspection, I knew that this was no accident, but someone had taken the liberty to slash my tire.

"Damn".

CHAPTER TWELVE

I made it back to my apartment after AAA Services responded to my roadside assistance. Luckily for me, the tow truck driver was not that far away from the gym when they came in. He towed me back to my house and even assisted me in changing out the ripped tire with the full-size spare I kept in the garage. By the time I arrived back at my place, Viv was nowhere to be found. To complicate matters, Evette pulled up just as the tow truck was pulling off. She had just returned from a weekend of wedding shopping with her girls. I would have hated for her to walk in on the continuation of last night's conversation with Vivian. The last thing I wanted to do today was reassure Evette that nothing was going on with Vivian, even though Viv had expressed other sentiments.

"Hey baby, how was Chicago? " I asked as she approached me, kissing my right cheek.

"It was OK," she responded, but her body language told me a different story.

"Well?" I probed a little more.

"Well, what?"

The defensive tone of her voice led me to believe that my instincts were correct. "I wouldn't know for sure, but usually brides to be ecstatic about finding the wedding dress of their dreams." I commented as I continued making my protein shake. Evette flopped down on the bar stool that faced me at the countertop island in the kitchen.

"The girls didn't like anything I tried on. Not even the dress I initially went to Chicago to see". She whined.

What did you think of the dresses? I quizzed.

"They were great, but the first dress my consultant chose for me to try on was my favorite".

Her humdrum disposition was lit up by the spark I saw in her. "Well, why don't we make plans for just you and I to go to Chicago. I'd love to see you in that dress." I replied with a smile.

"We can't do that," she snapped, adjusting herself on the stool.

"Says who? We can do whatever we want to do. And I want my baby to get the dress she wants. The wedding gown she deserves."

Evette smiled a half grin. "You would do that for me?"

"I would do that and so much more if you would let me." I commented as I stopped what I was doing and looked deep into her eyes so she could see that I was sincere in my words.

"But Bridgette and Sharmaine hated the dress. I want to look beautiful on my wedding day. I want a gown that will take everyone's breath away, especially yours."

"E, I hate to tell you this, but your girls are haters." I laughed. " There is no way my baby could ever look horrible. Besides, the only thing that matters is that you like the dress. Did you like the dress?"

"I loved it," she shyly responded, as if she was a little girl confessing her wish to Santa.

"Then that settles things. Me and you have a date in Chicago. Are you free this weekend?"

"You really want to take me?"

"I'll take that as a yes." I smiled as I walked around the kitchen island and planted a big wet kiss on her full lips. With that, Evette's entire demeanor changed. The cloud of gray lifted from across her face and she seemed more at ease.

"So, what did you do this weekend?" she asked as she took a seat beside me on the couch.

I paused. Honesty was the root of all good relationships. Along with trust, communication, honesty was a guiding principle I lived by, especially with Evette. I also knew if I told her everything that went down this weekend, including the conversation with Vivian, I would be setting myself up for a headache. It was Sunday. All I wanted was a relaxing day free of stress. I missed my lady. And the thought of getting her undressed and diving deep into her wet, warm oasis would all diminish if I told her the truth. So, I didn't, at least not at this moment.

"I didn't do much. Just hung out with the boys." I smiled, knowing that omitting the interaction with Vivian was for the best. " And missing my baby. Now, why don't you show me how much you missed me," I said as Evette climbed onto my lap smothering me with kisses as her hips gyrated, letting me know she did indeed miss me.

CHAPTER THIRTEEN

I made it to Wednesday, and I was already over this work week. My workload, which was usually manageable, had become a nuisance. Not only did we have two employees out on maternity leave, my big marketing campaign presentation for one of the top luxury brands was approaching. I wanted everything to be perfect. I was working long hours. The only stress relief was that Deshawn had been sexing me like crazy. Lord knows that man had big dick energy and enough stamina to back it up. He had dinner cooked for me when I arrived home. A bottle of my favorite wine and a hot bath was always awaiting my return. It was the small details that told me just how much he loved me. Even when I needed my space to throw myself into my work, Deshawn understood. He never complained. And as much as I hated asking him to leave, he hesitantly did. Him being in my presence was the best and worst distraction. Hell, your girl was always up for a good fuck, but Deshawn would have my ass going for hours. Before I knew it, it would be morning. I wouldn't get any work done.

So, when I told him I would be working late and not to bother cooking for me. I could tell he was a little disappointed. That didn't stop him from calling and texting to check up on me. Although my office was close to my home, Deshawn would always worry if I worked late. I had promised to text him when I left the office and as soon as I got home. I was heading out of the office. It was midnight. Time got the best of me. I had convinced Deshawn that I didn't need him to come escort me home. The elevator took me down to the parking garage. I made it to my car when my phone rang. Thinking it was Deshawn, I answered without noticing the unknown caller message display.

"Baby, I'm fine," I uttered.

"I wish I had told you that more when I had you," the familiar voice stated. His words struck my core. I paused just short of entering my vehicle. Grabbing for the door handle, I whispered, "Radir."

"Can we talk?"

"About what, Radir?" I asked, annoyed. " How did you get my number?"

"Sharmaine gave it to me. I can't stop thinking about you ever since I saw you. Can I come by?"

Everything inside me was screaming no, but my heart overpowered all logic and caved in as I whispered "Yes". I hung up the phone and climbed into my car. What had I agreed to? I knew Radir was the Satan. He was the demon that had to be expelled from my soul. He possessed me like an illness. Radir took me to heaven and the depths of hell. Why would I agree to seeing him? I was setting myself up for regret and a chance to dance with the devil. I prayed for strength and to keep my sanity for the whole seven minutes and sixteen seconds it took for me to drive home.

I pulled into the parking lot. I could feel my heart racing. It wasn't like the night in Chicago on the dance floor. We were in public. I drew courage and my toughness from those around me. Besides, what was the chance we would see each other again? Radir was my past. One that needed to stay there. But as I walked into the lobby, a flood of emotions resurfaced. I had drowned myself in holy water to rid myself of him, and there he was again. His rich, dark chocolate skin glowed under the LED lights. His dimples greeted me as he smiled upon my entrance. I felt all reason leave my body and my knees buckled under me. With steady breaths, I wanted to turn around and run, but was propelled toward him. Stopping just short of meeting him eighty percent of the way.

"Thank you for agreeing to meet me,"
"Why now, Radir?" I asked firmly.
"I don't know. I just. I mean.."
"You saw me happy. Living my life without you. Could that be it?" I yelled at him. There was an eerie silence between us.
"Can I come up and we talk in private?," he asked.

I had played it cool until now. I should never be alone with him. At least we had the company of the new security guard in the lobby with us. Being alone with Radir would weaken my already low immune system to him. I felt the buzzing of my phone. I knew it was Deshawn and that should have snapped me out of the trance I was in. But it didn't. Even when the security guard asked if everything was ok. I had time to say no and walk away, but I didn't. Instead, I agreed to let Radir up into my condo. A place where peace and serenity existed. And now I was welcoming the devil into my space to roam free again.

We rode the elevator in silence. The elevator stopped on the seventh floor, and we strolled down to the end of the hallway. I opened the door and allowed Radir to enter. I put my belongings down on the table in the foyer. Radir was about ten steps ahead of me, surveying my surroundings. I could smell his cologne wafting through my place. He had five minutes to explain himself. That was all I could endure. I was already playing with fire. Anything more I was sure was leading to brimstone and damnation.

"So talk. You have five minutes," I said, trying to play it cool.

"I know we left things unsettled between us. I'm so sorry,"

"Unsettled! You left me, no, you cheated on me with that bitch! You didn't even have the courtesy to tell me it was over! You just ghosted me like a coward. Changed your phone number, moved and blocked me on social media. That's not unsettled. That's fucking making me look like a fool." I yelled.

"Baby, I'm so sorry. I didn't mean to hurt you. I just.."

"You just what? Oh, let me guess. You realized she wasn't me. Yea, she might have been skinnier, maybe even prettier, but she would never love you like I did. So why are you here? Where is she at? Why are you not laying up with her instead of calling me?" I cried out as I walked away from him. I felt his presence directly behind me. He was close enough for me to feel his shallow breath on my neck. The warmth of his body covered me like the heat from hell. I couldn't turn around. I couldn't allow him to see the hurt that still resided in me after all this time. I prayed he didn't touch me. I was too weak to resist.

"I miss you. I missed you the moment I left. I just didn't know how to tell you. I regretted it. When I saw you in Chicago, it reminded me of what I gave up. I've grown up since then. That superficial shit doesn't mean shit to me. I miss your curves, your lips and hips, the sound of you moaning for me and the way you made a nigga feel. I can't lie. I've been with a few women since we broke up, but none of them could compare to you. That's why I'm here. That's why I drove all this way. Begged your friend for your number. I wanted you to know that you weigh heavy on my mind, my heart and my dick."

My heart palpitations and the closeness in proximity to the only person I truly loved made my palms sweaty and caused a nervousness to sweep over me. He just stood behind me. I imagined him wanting me the way I had yearned for him throughout the years. My vivaciousness was now something he craved. I felt my heart beating in my chest as he took hold of my neck with his left hand and swiped my hair to the side so he could kiss away the silence that had taken over the room. Radir had moved close enough that our breathing and heartbeat were now in sync, a connection that I once relished in.

"Ray, I can't." I whispered, as I attempted to regain control of the situation.

"You can. I know you missed me too," he moaned as his lips traveled the familiar route of my body. I watched as his tongue and lips glided over my clothes and traced an outline for him to travel. His teeth pulling at my garments, begging me to unravel myself and give in to him. I closed my eyes, praying for the willpower to step away. To remove myself from Satan's rapturous hold on me, I tried to think of what's his name, but shit, I couldn't even remember his name. I was engaged to... again, I couldn't think of who my heart was supposed to belong to. I had become easy prey to this venomous creature and emotions from the past. In one embrace, Radir had wiped my present away and conjured up all of the things I left in the past. And at this moment, I want to live in that memory.

Radir pressed his manly agent against me as he held on to my thickness. His tongue marched in and out of my mouth like we were at war. I took hold of it and tugged as the battle began. I wasn't sure when or how, but we were both standing in the living room, naked. The lights of the city skyline danced around our bodies as he held me close enough for his erect penis to slide in and out of my wet thighs. That was the prelude of what was to come. I tried with every rational bone in my body to stop what was about to happen, but the past crept up on me. Old feelings and memories clouded my heart as Radir slipped his enlarged phallus into my sanctuary.

My moans led me down an array of passionate nights and explosive entanglements from my past relationship with Radir. I was on a fast track to hell in the most pleasurable and ultimately regrettable journey. I couldn't stop the ride now, as Radir and I were in a full-on grinding session. Him pounding me into submission and me reliving how good his dick felt inside of me. Not once did I back away from his thrust. Not once did I hesitate to cum for him. It felt so right, and yet, I knew I should have ended it. And without warning, Radir climaxed, deep in my warmth. In our haste, we didn't strap up. The rawness of his throbbing veins and the thickness of his engorged head caused me to throw caution to the wind and, along with it, my sanity. I knew better. But he felt so good.

We lay there in our birthday suits, our bodies covered in the mist of sweat caused from our bodies colliding. We didn't say a word. We allowed our bodies to say it all as we fucked for hours. It was round one, then round two and finally ending at the third time I allowed Radir's curved magic stick to cast a spell on me. I was indeed tangled up in a dangerous web. The devil had a hold on me, and I wasn't so sure I wanted him to let me go.

CHAPTER FOURTEEN

Evette had buried herself in her work. We hardly saw each other over the past few weeks. Her career was something I knew was important to her. I preferred not to be a distraction to her. I didn't know how to take that, particularly since I had seen her work under a tight deadline previously. The uniqueness of this project compared to the previous ones was lost on me. But I gave her some space as she requested.

The only good thing about Evette needing space was it gave me an opportunity to run errands I had neglected. I completed some projects at home and assisted my sister with a few tasks. I had to run up to Grand Rapids to pick up a few things. My intention was to be in and out. I didn't make it a habit of being in my old stomping ground. There was too much history and just as many demons haunting me there. It was best that I stay away from the city if I could help it. But since I was going to be downtown during the afternoon hours, I falsely reasoned that I would be ok.

I had been walking through the crowded streets of the city, lost in thought, when I heard a familiar voice call out to me.

"Hey, Deshawn! Long time no see!"

I turned around to see a man approaching me, dressed in designer street gear and a scar above his eyebrow. I immediately recognized him. Cam and I used to run the streets together. Hell, one might even say we were family. Back in my younger days, Cam was my right-hand man. Together, we built a drug empire that supplied everything north of Interstate 94 and west of Lansing. Our small-time operation was big time for us. Between the money and the women, you couldn't tell us anything. We had more power than we knew what to do with and just as many enemies as our presence and operation grew.

I could never prove it, but I was sure that Cam had set me up to take the fall for being a drug kingpin. The way it all went down, there was no way the DEA could have known what they knew unless they had a man on the inside. Despite all the money I had acquired, I wasn't a flashy nigga. Yeah, I had two cars. My home was modest and my gear was always on point. I had seen enough fools get taken down by showing off and spending absurd amounts of money, buying expensive cars, jewelry, and clothing. All of that was nothing but a magnet to attract attention from the authorities.

It was weird how I got busted and Cam didn't. In fact, he inherited the kingdom. I wasn't mad. I had done my time at the top. At first, Cam kept his promise and my commissary stayed stacked. But when you doing a fifteen-year bid, anything can happen. Eventually, the visits slowed down until there were no more. And the money on my books, let's just say it wasn't as plentiful as when I started. I had heard through the grapevine that Cam was the top dog. But I knew that nigga was living off my name and what I built. I should have been mad, but I wasn't. By that time, I had changed my perspective on the drug game. I had all the time I needed to think about every choice I ever made, every bullet I ever fired, and every soul I altered. I was making changes. Changes that did not involve my grimy past. I had already done a quarter of my life behind bars, behind my stupidity. The next chapter of my life did not include anything or anyone from my past life. Vivian was the only exception.

I stood there; eyes locked on Cam as he made his way over to me.

"Cam? Is that you?" I asked, my eyes narrowing as I took a step back.

"The one and only," Cam said with a smirk, his eyes scanning me up and down. "You're looking good, man. What you been up to?"

"Nothing that concerns you," I said.

Cam's smirk disappeared and his expression turned serious. "Actually, it does concern you. I need your help."

I raised an eyebrow. "My help? What kind of help?"

"Fam, I've gotten myself into some trouble," Cam admitted, his eyes darting around nervously. "I owe some people a lot of money, and they not happy bout it. I need someone to help me get out of this mess, and I thought of you."

This nigga. I shook my head. "I'm aint interested in getting involved in yo mess, Cam. You made your bed, now lie in it."

Cam's expression hardened. "You owe me, Deshawn. Remember all those times I covered for you when you screwed up? When I took the fall for you? You owe me."

I felt a pang of guilt in my chest. Cam was right - we had been in the same gang together. Cam and I had done our fair share of dirt, but I didn't owe him shit. All we shared now was the past. The Deshawn he wanted no longer existed. That was a lifetime ago, and I had moved on.

"I don't owe you a damn thing, Cam. I'm sorry you're in trouble, but you'll have to find someone else to help you."

Cam's expression turned to anger. "Fine," he spat. "But don't come crying to me when you need help someday. You're nothing without us, Deshawn. Don't forget that."

I watched as Cam stormed off into the crowd, feeling a mix of relief and guilt. I made the right decision. Nothing good came from living in my past and that included allowing Cam back into my life.

CHAPTER FIFTEEN

My guilt about sleeping with Radir had only intensified in the days following our encounter. I couldn't shake the feeling that I had betrayed Deshawn. It had taken me years to find happiness again and in minutes, I gave it all up and for what? The same pain I'd exasperatedly tried to escape from. My chest hurt. I had to tell someone, and Sharmaine and Bridgette were the first people who came to mind.

It was no secret that both of them didn't really care for Deshawn. They couldn't get over his shady past. All they knew was he was a felon. They couldn't see anything past that which was sad because Deshawn was everything I wanted in a partner, minus the rap sheet. He was a hard worker and loyal. And outside of Radir, was the only man whose hose watered my garden just right. Deshawn loved me. And I thought I was in love with him. Until Radir reappeared...

Sharmaine and Bridgette felt the same about Radir. They were there for me through all the drama with him. The only thing Radir had going for him was his executive title and his strong six figure salary. We had history. A past that was good when it was good. But it was also bad and toxic. The events from the other night weighed heavy on me. Just thinking about what that man did to me caused a rush of emotions and my panties to become wet.

I needed to figure this shit out before it got out of hand. I wanted nothing more than to be Deshawn's wife, but the sex with Radir was a spell I could not break free from. This secret was eating me up. Against my better judgement, I called Bridgett and Sharmaine. I need some advice and a neutral setting away from the apartment to get my mind right. Hell, every time I walked by the wall of windows in the front room, I thought about all the things I did with Radir. Things that signed my entry into hell.

As I sat across from them in the café, I took a deep breath and prepared to share my secret.

"Guys, I have something to tell you," I began hesitantly. "I... I slept with someone."

Sharmaine and Bridgette looked at me, surprised, but didn't say anything.

"It was Radir," I continued, my voice barely above a whisper. "He's in town. We hooked up and one thing lead to another."

Sharmaine and Bridgette both gasped in unison, their eyes widening.

"Radir? I just know you lying bitch?" Sharmaine asked, her voice barely concealing her excitement.

I nodded, feeling a flush rise to my cheeks. "I don't know what came over me. It was a mistake, and I feel terrible about it."

Bridgette put a comforting hand on my arm. "Gurrl, you ain't married yet. You don't know what your felon be doing when he not around."

Sharmaine leaned in, her eyes sparkling with curiosity. "Okay, spill the tea. How was it?"

I blushed even deeper but found myself unable to resist the urge to share the details. "It was amazing. Time and age improved his pipe game a hunit percent."

Sharmaine and Bridgette both giggled in response, clearly enjoying the juicy gossip.

But as the conversation continued, my guilt only grew. I couldn't stop thinking about Deshawn and how devastated he would be if he found out. I had to end things with Radir, but I wasn't sure I wanted to.

"I don't know what to do," I admitted. "I can't keep doing this, but I don't want to stop."

Bridgette nodded sympathetically. "Listen, you know I can't stand Radir. I'm not a huge fan of Deshawn, but he loves you. You gonna do you regardless of what I say. Just be careful, boo."

Sharmaine chimed in. "And if I can be honest, Radir hurt you bad. The dick might be good, but at what cost? I don't have to like who you be with, but they better treat you right or else. Radir ain't that one. Hell, Deshawn might not be the one either, but if he makes you happy, the felon is ok with me."

I nodded slowly, feeling a sense of relief wash over me. I knew it wouldn't be easy, but I was determined to do the right thing. Sharmaine was right, Radir played me bad. He was an EX for a reason. Deshawn had done nothing but love me and love on me. There was no reason for me to play the field. Shit, Deshawn even put a ring on it and there was no reason for me to mess around on him. This pussy belonged to him. I just needed to remind her that next time I was around Radir.

It was finally the weekend, and I couldn't wait to spend some quality time with Deshawn. We had been planning to ride to

Chicago to pick out my wedding dress ever since the fiasco with the girl's weekend. I almost wished I had just taken Deshawn with me from the very beginning. Maybe then I wouldn't have run into Radir. Maybe then everything that had happened since then would be a figment of my imagination. It had been an entire week since I spent any quality time with Deshawn. This getaway with him was much needed. I needed to be around him and covered in his love. Without him around, my trust in myself faltered. I often think that if I had allowed him to come escort me home that night, it would have been Deshawn making love to me instead of Radir.

As we hit the road, my cell phone began to ring incessantly. At first, I tried to ignore it, claiming it was work-related. Deshawn, being the understanding partner he was, told me he didn't mind if I needed to take the call. But I knew that if I answered the phone, I would blow my cover. Radir's number flashed across my home screen. I had been avoiding Radir's calls all week, knowing that if Deshawn found out about him, it would only cause more problems. The close proximity of the car meant that if I answered, Deshawn would undoubtedly hear Radir's voice on the other end. And nothing he had to talk about was work related.

After several minutes of the phone ringing, I couldn't take it anymore. I needed to answer and put an end to Radir's persistent calls. Picking up the phone, I tried to sound as composed as possible.

"Hello. What do you need?" I asked, trying to keep my voice steady.

"I need your pussy juices all over my face." Radir coyly replied.

My heart sank. His words went right to my garden. A gush of warmness coated my private, as if to welcome his request. I knew that if Radir's words had this type of reaction on me, there was no way in hell I could see him anytime soon, or eva. It would only lead to trouble, and I had already risked enough.

"I'm sorry. I'm away for the weekend. I'm on my way to pick up my wedding dress. I really can't talk about the campaign right now. Can we discuss this later?" I asked, hoping that Radir would take the hint.

"So you're with him? And you're in Chicago? Great. I'll see you later." Radir said, before hanging up.

Radir hung up the phone before I could even respond

I let out a sigh of relief. I knew that Radir's persistence wasn't going to stop anytime soon, but for now, I could focus on enjoying her weekend with Deshawn. I put my phone away and turned to Deshawn, smiling.

"Sorry about that. Let's focus on us for now, okay?" I said, reaching out to hold his hand.

Deshawn smiled back, squeezing my hand gently. "Of course, Evette. You and me, that's all that matters."

I smiled, believing every word he said. I turned the music back up and we jammed to sounds of old school hip hop and R&B from the 90's as we rode to Chicago.

CHAPTER SIXTEEN

Deshawn and I spent the day browsing different bridal boutiques in Chicago, trying on various wedding dresses until we finally found the perfect one. I couldn't believe how lucky I was to have Deshawn by my side during the dress shopping process. Just knowing that he had my back and supported my decision was everything I missed out on when I was here with my girlfriends. Although he was there in the boutique with me, he honored my request to not come into the fitting room. I wanted to keep the surprise of seeing me in my dress on our wedding day special.

As we left the boutique, Deshawn suggested we have dinner in downtown Chicago. We found a romantic restaurant with a view of the city skyline. The ambiance of the restaurant added to the success of today's activities. I finally had a wedding gown. And to top things off, Deshawn paid for it. I told him I had it, but he insisted on paying for it. The dress was over my initial budget. I knew I could afford it, but I wasn't sure how Deshawn could afford my expensive taste. So, when his card swiped and approved, I breathed a sigh of relief. I knew at some point we needed to talk about our finances. I didn't want any surprises when it came to differences in pay or how I spent my money once we were married. The only plus was Deshawn owned his own home. If needed, he could sell that to help us out. I hope he didn't think I would be financing this marriage. But that was a conversation for another day. Right now, Deshawn was spoiling your girl, and I needed every ounce of love, attention and dime he was showering me with.

We enjoyed each other's company over a delicious meal and talked about our future together. As we finished our meal, my phone rang, interrupting the romantic ambiance. It was Radir, calling again. I hesitated, wondering whether or not to answer, but eventually decided to excuse myself from the table and take the call outside.

"Radir, I thought I made it clear that I didn't want to talk. I'm on a date with my fiancé," I said, trying to sound firm.

"But you're thinking about me," Radir replied, sounding arrogant.

I was becoming frustrated. I had been looking forward to this night with Deshawn, and now Radir was ruining it with his persistent calls.

"Radir, I can't do this right now. I'll call you tomorrow," I said, before hanging up.

I took a deep breath and tried to shake off the annoyance I felt. As I walked back into the restaurant, Deshawn looked up and smiled at me.

"Everything okay?" he asked, concern etched on his face.

I forced a smile. "Yeah, just work stuff. Let's enjoy the rest of our night."

We ended our meal with dessert, holding hands and laughing as we caught up on the past week's activities. I attempted to forget all about Radir and his enticing comments. I focused on the love and joy I felt being with Deshawn.

Deshawn and I ended the night in the Jacuzzi tub in the suite of our hotel room. The smell of roses and the sparkling flickers of light from the candles relaxed my mind and mood as I leaned into Deshawn's muscular arms. The bubbles and heat from the water soothed all the stress away. Deshawn kissed and massaged my shoulders as I sat between his legs. I could feel the girth of his manhood pressing against my backside. Lord knows I wanted to climb on top of his throbbing stick and ride him into the night but I couldn't, knowing that I had unprotected sex with Radir.

My poor decisions had me looking unappreciative of everything that Deshawn had done for me. We both knew we wanted each other. I just couldn't take the chance. I needed to be checked out. The last thing I wanted to do was ask Deshawn to strap up. We haven't used condoms in over a year. And I wasn't about to cause concern by asking him to do so now. I just needed to buy some time. My doctor's appointment was on Tuesday. For now, I'll have to find an alternative way to make him happy. I knew just the thing to do, and I knew Deshawn would love that I asked instead of him.

The sexual tension had me in a vice grip. Deshawn's hands had traveled my wet body and outlined all the places he wanted to visit. He was stirring up all kinds of emotions and my inner sanctuary in between my thighs was more than ready for some action. I needed to release. If for nothing else, to prove that Deshawn could erase any trace of Radir. The rush of heat that emanated from all the fondling and groping gave me the courage to whisper in Deshawn's ear, "I want you to fuck me.. In my ass."

"Oh, shit!" Deshawn whispered, surprised at my request.

I could tell he was shocked and excited that I was finally ready for him to have me in this way. It was something that was a firm no before. But I wanted him. No one had enjoyed me before. It may have also been the guilt spurring this extreme request, but I couldn't back out now. If I didn't allow him to penetrate me this way, he certainly would be expecting to enter me another way. And considering my indiscretions, I couldn't allow that to happen.

The soapy water helped to guide Deshawn into my tight opening. He was gentle in the way he entered me. Slowly, he forced the tip of his enlarged shaft into me. I took a deep breath, exhaled and relaxed, something that Bridgett had disclosed to me once in conversation. This technique was supposed to make the penetration tolerable. And it did. The pressure was so intense that after a few strokes; I had to pull away. Deshawn held me in his arms.

"Are you sure, baby?" he questioned. Concerned at my quick dismount.

"Yes," I whispered, giving him the green light to slowly repeat the process. This time, I allowed my body to absorb the intense sensation of his magic stick. I gasped as my tight opening stretched to accommodate Deshawn's growth. I slowly and awkwardly moved my hips on top of him allowing my body to become accustomed to what was happening. Deshawn's hands were gripping my waist as we matched each other's stride. My soft moans rang out as the water splashed around us. Deshawn buried his face in my breast as he tugged at my nipples and sucked on my titties. To my surprise, I was enjoying my ride. My virgin opening was extra sensitive. I could feel every inch of Deshawn as he moved in and out of me. I wanted him to fuck me back into his arms and take away my guilt. As the water splashed about the tub and onto the bathroom floor, I could tell he was all for fucking me too. Except I was fucking out of guilt and he was fucking me out of love.

I woke up to my vibrating phone on the nightstand. The bright light from the home screen flashed. There was a message from Radir. I looked over at Deshawn, who was sound asleep. His snores drowned out any noise I could make. I took my phone off of the charger and read the text message.

> **Radir–**
> Evette R U Up?

> **Radir–**
> Evette room 716.

The last message was left thirty minutes ago. The time on my phone read 2:35am. I looked over at Deshawn. He was rocked. He had a satisfied look on his face, which he rightfully earned. Against my better judgement, I replied.

> **Me–**
> Radir leave me alone.

I saw the bubbles appear on the screen. And within seconds, Radir replied.

> **Radir–**
> Room 716

I took another look at Deshawn. He was sound asleep. I shook my head, thinking that I had to put an end to this bullshit with Radir. How did he know where we were staying? Why was he following me? I couldn't allow this shit to go on any further. Slipping on a t-shirt and leggings, I grabbed my sneakers and slowly opened the door.

I lightly knocked on the door to room 716. Radir quickly opened the wooden door and pulled me into the room.

"Evette, I can't stop thinking about you," Radir said, his voice thick with emotion.

My heart dropped. I couldn't believe Radir was confessing his feelings for me, especially at such an inappropriate hour and after all this time.

"Radir, I can't do this. I'm in a relationship. I have to go," I said as I tried to grab the room door. Radir pulled me into him and planted a deep, wet kiss on my lips. His tongue parted my neutral-colored lips and welcomed him in as I bit down on it. Before I knew it, Radir had pulled my leggings down and planted kisses on my thighs. His fingers strummed my prize box as if it was his to claim. My stickiness covered his fingers as he slid in and out of me.

"Tell me you want me," Radir's dry voice echoed in the dark room.

I could only moan out loud as I attempted to fight off Radir's gestures. But I couldn't. Radir knew me and my body and I missed the way he made me feel. My resistance finally gave in when Radir drowned himself deep into my puddles of wetness. His tongue licked the combination of old and new juices that covered me. Just hours ago, Deshawn had torn me open, causing me to explode from both orifices. And now Radir was enjoying the fruits of Deshawn's labor.

I couldn't stop him. I just forced his head into my curves as he bathed in my juices. Radir loved on me as my body stayed pinned to the wall. All I had to give; he took with his tongue. I moaned with each flick and twist as my body shook from his oral stimulation. Every vibration from his tongue sent my flower exploding as if I had pollinated his mouth. I was weak with disgust and just as satisfied. Why was I still so weak for this man? I thought to myself as he stood up from his gardening session and faced me with his eyes locked on me. Radir leaned in and kissed me with all scents smothering his face. It turned me on as I inhaled my essence as our lips collided.

I was tired, confused, and sexually satisfied. My state was equally shared between both men in my life. One I knew loved me and would do me right. The other one who could give me the life I had always pictured and on paper, we were compatible and sustainable. Why was this so hard? Deshawn was what I needed. Radir was what I always wanted. And as I headed back to my hotel room, I prayed I would choose correctly. I swiped the plastic room key across the keypad to the door. I slowly opened the door, hoping not to wake Deshawn. To my surprise, he was still resting peacefully. I wanted to jump in the bed beside him and pretend that what I just allowed to happen didn't happen. But the guilt of what I allowed Radir to do wouldn't allow me the rest I needed, nor the kind of love I deserved.

"Good morning, beautiful," Deshawn greeted me.

"Good Morning" I replied with a half-smile. I never went back to sleep. I spent the last few hours thinking about Deshawn and Radir. Here I was with the man I was engaged to, yet I was allowing my past fuck up to insult my emotional intelligence. Radir was my past. He had proven that he was incapable of loving me the way I deserved to be loved and cherished. I knew all of that and still, I ended up messing around with him not once, but on two separate occasions. I needed to get my shit together. My mind was so occupied that I didn't notice Deshawn approaching me from behind.

He put his arm around me and pulled me close.

"Everything okay?" he asked, his voice full of concern.

I looked up at him and smiled, feeling grateful for his presence in my life.

"Everything's okay. I'm just glad I have you," I said, leaning in for a kiss. Thankful that I could shower last night's shame off of me.

Deshawn kissed me back. His soft lips were gentle to the touch. I could feel his love for me in our embrace. I wanted to stay in this space for as long as I could. It was the only place I felt safe. The only time I trusted myself to do the right thing. Deshawn's kisses intensified. I welcomed his outpour of affection. And before long, Deshawn had slipped my clothes off me and, without thinking about what would happen next, Deshawn's love stick entered my throbbing walls. I welcomed him in with a moan and an oh shit. He took it as a sign that I missed him, but really it was an oh shit, what have I done?

CHAPTER SEVENTEEN

"Man, I can't believe you brought the dress," Greg sighed.
"I told you clowns; Evette is the woman for me. There isn't anything I wouldn't do for her. Besides, I had the cash for it, so it wasn't an inconvenience. I spoke up.

" I bet she just loved that shit. Women love counting our pockets," Greg laughed as we finished up lunch.

"Mike, tell this dude to stop dating from the bottom of the barrel." I laughed. "Evette has her own money, there is no need for her to be worried about my pockets. Hell, she doesn't even know just how deep my shit run."

"So, you haven't told her?" Mike chimed in as he looked back at me. We were heading to the sanitation truck to finish up our Monday route.

"It's never come up. I know at some point I'll let her know."

"So, you got homegirl out here thinking she marrying someone who barely makes fifty stacks, and you a whole millionaire. How you think she gonna react when she finds out?" Greg asked.

"First, I know Evette loves me for me. My past is just that, my past. I put that money aside because there's no retirement plan or 401k's for drug dealers. That nest egg was one of the bright spots of doing that bid. I knew whenever I got out, I wouldn't have to go back to the streets." I explained.

"You were one of the smart ones." Echoed Mike.

"Yeah, but the smart part comes if I live long enough to enjoy it." I said, thinking of my recent encounter with Cam.

"Facts! No cap, my nigga. The game ain't what it used to be and your ass has outlived most scenarios of that lifestyle.

"I know, and my plan is to keep living, and that includes having Evette in my life." I added as Mike climbed into the cabin of the truck. The engine turned on just as Greg and I reached for the handles. We took our designated post, holding on tight as the truck pulled off. We had one of the few remaining routes that required three people to man it. The stack of houses and duplexes that lined the street left little room to garages or private parking spaces, leaving the residents to park on the street. The garbage truck's mechanical arm couldn't always reach the trash bins because of the heavily packed streets, so they tasked us to manually pull in the bins. It didn't matter to me. I had a job and good company.

I didn't even mind Greg and Mike giving me grief over my relationship with Evette. I knew they were just old school with an old school player mentality. But that money conversation at lunch strung a cord. I wasn't hiding the fact that I had money. It just never came up in conversation. Evette had her own money plus a six-figure career with a title. She didn't blink twice when I told her about my job. It really didn't matter. Whenever we went out, I paid the bill. Evette never came out-of-pocket even when her triflin friends tagged along. Maybe it was time Evette and I have the finance conversation. Maybe it would clear up questions she may have about me really wanting to take care of her.

We finished up the route. The truck pulled into the main truck docking station just before five. I dapped Mike and Greg up before heading into the locker room. I got distracted by a few other guys, said my good byes, and headed out to my truck. Immediately, my stance and stride stiffened up as I saw the image of Cam standing by my truck. I couldn't make a scene, but this fool was beggin for me to come unglued. All that thinking for a change shit I learned in prison had me fucked up. It didn't prepare you for situations like this. Staring the devil in his face wasn't a required chapter to complete.

"What up Doe? " Cam's evil smirk played on his face as the toothpick hung in the corner of his lips.

"What up?" I replied as our eyes locked.

"I had to come see this shit for myself. I heard you were a garbage man. I thought my mans was lying. I guess I owe his as a stack. Look at you, clockin out smelling like shit." He joked. "This can't be the great DeShawn that once ruled all of western Michigan."

"Is there something I can help you with?"

"Naw, man, but I certainly can help you out."

"I'm not interested in nothing you have to offer me."

"C'mon. I know this ain't the lifestyle you want. A player like you, once king of the streets, now hustling trash." Cam laughed.

"What is your point?"

"My point is you know you belong in the city with me. It could be just like the old days. You could be my right hand. We could be brothers again. Cause this shit ain't it. I know you want back in." Cam stated with confidence.

"I hate to burst your bubble, but I'm good. I told you that when you approached me in downtown Grand Rapids." I firmly replied.

"Look here .." Cam started to speak before I cut him off.

No, you look here. I'm not that same nigga. The fact that I been out of the system for three years now, and this the first time you came checking for me, tells me everything I need to know about our brotherhood. I'mma pass on anything you have to say to me."

"I hope that fine thick ass lady of yours knows she got a real one." Cam said with a wicked grin on his face. As soon as he mentioned Evette, I felt my core burn as my jaw tightened. The muscles in my face hardened as I rushed Cam without giving a second thought about who at my work saw my actions.

"You go anywhere near her and I'll kill you," I whispered in his ear as I yoked him up against my truck.

"Now, that's the nigga I know. Yea, get mad. I knew you had it in you. The Deshawn I know is still in there. Just beggin to come on out." Cam laughed as he fixed himself once I released my hold on him. "I'mma see you. "Yea, I'mma see you again," Cam smirked as he walked away. I watched as he climbed into the smoke-colored Range Rover with dark tinted windows.

Cam always knew how to provoke me. He knew I didn't take kindly to anyone messing with my girl. Back in the day I would drop a nigga if he looked at my girl the wrong way. It seems Cam has been doing his homework. I knew the moment we ran into each other; I wasn't going to shake him off easy. But Cam was delusional. We hadn't been brothers since those steel doors closed behind me. The old me died when I realized I had two options in life: Keep playing in the streets waiting for the bullet that was meant for me and end up dead or change my life around and start living. I had already hit bottom. Prison will have a man thinking about every missed step, poor decision and regrettable moment you ever lived through. I had twenty-five years to relive them all. Not once did I ever see myself at my age going back to the streets. Hustling is a young man's sport. The rules have changed. The code ain't the same. And I could never play second to anyone.

Cam had me on defense. No, I wasn't giving him too much thought. But him showing me his hand told me that nigga was desperate and desperate people are reckless. Cam had never been one to plan out anything. His actions were usually the result of in the moments emotions. He took one look at me on the street and allowed all the memories and emotions associated with the past to resurface. We hadn't seen each other in over twenty years. He stopped visiting after the fifth year I went in. Even then, the last three, he only made the ride once or twice a year. But we were supposed to be brothers. That brother shit only applies to you when you in a nigga's sightline. The minute they don't see you on a daily basis you become an afterthought. Sad to say, I don't blame him. Life goes on. Time don't wait for no one. But I know for a fact, we were tighter than that. Had the shoe been on the other foot? I would have held Cam down. Visits and money. I would have been the first person to greet him when he got out. That's the type of brother I am.

I had a lot of time to analyze my relationship with Cam in prison. Looking back, I was a true friend to him. He was my family. I think I took for granted that Cam felt the same way about me. Jealousy often hides behind the guise of terms like family and friendship. Images of his face and reactions often replayed in my mind. He was never really happy for me, even though we were partners. That same look on his face was the same evil smirk he showed back up with. He didn't have my back. He just went along for the ride until he saw an opportunity to take it all. When he stopped taking my calls and the visits became less, it all clicked for me. Truth be told, I was glad he cut me off while I was locked up. Lord knows where I would be if he had been the brother I thought he was.

I hadn't spoken to anyone from the old crew since being released. I hadn't planned on it either. Most of them were dead, in prison, or cracked out. Not a life I wanted to be associated with. Now I have my past confronting me after all this time. The only person I was comfortable talking to about this was Vivian. She was the only person who understood that side of me. But I hadn't spoken with her since that night she pulled up on me. I desperately needed my friend right now, but I wasn't sure she was ready to accept that this was all we could be. Hell, she had a whole family. There wasn't anything she could offer me once she told me she was getting married. My heart broke into a million pieces that day and there wasn't a damn thing I could do about it. I didn't even beg her not to. I was doing serious time, and like I said, life moves on without you when you're locked up. It would have been selfish of me to think she would wait for me, but you can't fault me for wishing.

CHAPTER EIGHTEEN

Vivian agreed to meet me for lunch at our favorite hangout spot. I arrived ten minutes early and waited inside the restaurant. I watched as the woman I once was head over heels for enter the establishment. The hostess escorted her over to my table. Vivian was wearing a stylish blazer, tank top, and a pair of cutoff fringed denim shorts that showed off her long legs. I always admired the way Vivian dressed. It was street, classy and sexy at the same time. When we were together, she was the trendsetter for all the girls in the neighborhood. They all wanted to be her. Her confidence stayed on ten and her walk alone had men everywhere watching her. It was no different today than it was all those years ago, as all eyes were on her as she sat down at the table.

What's up, Viv?

"Hey Deshawn," she said shyly.

"What's with all the formalities, girl?" I joked. Vivian usually greeted me with a hug and a kiss on the cheek. Both of which were replaced by a distant stare. "Common girl, It's me."

"Deshawn, the last time we spoke, you made it very clear to me where we stand."

"Viv. We have a lot of history. That night when you came by the last thing I thought you were going to tell me was that you still had feelings for me." There was a long pause before I carefully crafted my next words. "Listen Viv, Imma always have love for you. But you and I both have moved on. You did what you thought you needed to do and, well; I have to live with the consequences of my actions. There is one thing I know for sure: I can't live without you in my corner. I need you, Viv. I need you as a friend. Are you ok with that?" I asked. Vivian lifted her head and our eyes locked. She shook her head as she mouthed "Yes,"

I smiled as her facial muscles relaxed. Our waitress joined us and politely took our orders. As we chatted, I wished things had been different between Vivian and I. I was young and dumb. Every discussion I'd made in life at that point had been questionable. The only thing I was ever certain about was my love for her. I always thought it would be me and her till the very end. Hell, I even allowed myself to imagine the white picket fence and house with kids. That dream still holds true. I loved Vivian; I was just not in love with her anymore. It took fifteen good years to get her out of my system. Her friendship was something no one could take away from me. It was the one thing I knew I could count on. As the conversation continued, I could tell that Vivian was comfortable always having that part of my heart.

I told her about my recent encounter with Cam. There was a shocked look on her face as I told her what had transpired.

"You need to be careful, Deshawn. Cam is not the same person we grew up with" Vivian warned.

"Look Viv, I couldn't care less who Cam is now or was before. He is a part of my past that needs to stay there. I can handle him. I want you to be careful. That nigga has been traveling down here more frequently. I don't want him coming for you to get to me. So if he approaches you, I need to know." I stated. It didn't matter that we were not a couple. Vivian held a special place in my heart, and I would protect her at any cost.

Vivian shook her head in acknowledgement of my words. We finished up lunch. I gave her the same warm hug I had embraced her after all these years. I walked her to her car and watched as she drove off. In those minutes, I saw the maturity in me and her. There was a time I wouldn't have let her go. But there was a difference in loving someone and being in love. The only woman for me was Evette. But Vivian, I loved her. And nothing would take that away from me.

CHAPTER NINETEEN

―✦✦✦―

It was presentation day. I was nervous but as prepared as I could be. It didn't matter how many people would be present to hear my pitch, the only person I had to impress was the client. The conference room was all set up. I was expecting a roomful of executives, the team from Melanated Cosmetics and a few of my colleagues. I had set up the virtual presentation for the Hong Kong executives and made sure that the material had been delivered and was set up on their end. The makeup artist and models were setting up and getting ready to show off their skills. I had supplied them with branded merchandise to wear, so the presentation had a unified look. The only thing left for me to do was calm my nerves.

Just as I was getting ready, Tamika, my assistant, buzzed me.
"Yes, Tamika?"
"You have a visitor"
"Can you be a little more specific?"
"Yes." She chuckled. "There is an incredibly handsome man out here with flowers for you.

"Thank you," I said sarcastically. Images of DeShawn swept across my mind. " Let Him in," I responded. When I turned to face the opening door, to my surprise, it was Radir.

"What are you doing here?" I whispered as I rushed over to close the door behind him.

"Hey baby. Is That any way to greet someone who came all this way bearing flowers?" he joked.

"I am not your baby, Radir. You have no right being here uninvited." I sternly stated. Although my eyes and heart said something different. "You need to leave. Now."

"I just stopped by to give you some good luck wishes. Here, these are for you. Your presentation is today, right?"

"Yes, and now is not the time. You can't be here Radir"

"Listen I know your busy, let me take you out tonight to celebrate."

'Radir, I can't. We can't. You need to leave now." I warned.

"Not until you say you will have dinner with me." He said, holding my hands in his. The smell of his cologne and the image of him wearing that custom made suit had me hypnotized.

"I ca-..."

"I will stand here until you say yes," Radir stated, looking deep into my eyes.

"Fine. Text me the time and location. Now, leave." I said as I opened the door and watched as Radir slyly walked out of my office with a devilish grin on his face. No sooner than the door closed behind Radir, Tamika buzzed me again.

"You have another guest," she chuckled." I'll send him back"

I opened the door and was about to scream what now, when to my surprise, it was Deshawn holding a bouquet of my favorite flowers, pink Calla Lilies.

"Is everything alright baby? " He asked as he closed the door behind him.

"It is now that you are here." I said, falling into his open arms. The warmth of his embrace eased away the tension of Radir, but not the imagery.

'Listen, I know that you are busy. I just wanted to bring the most beautiful woman in the world some flowers for her big day."

"You didn't need to bring them all this way. You could have had them delivered. Shouldn't you be at work?"

"Yeah, the boys are parked out front. I took my jumpsuit off downstairs before coming up. But if I had the flowers delivered, then I wouldn't see how stunning you look today. Turn around for me one time."

I blushed as I indulged Deshawn and his request.

"Damn Ma, that ass looking real good in that dress. Now that you're not working on your presentation, hopefully you'll have some time for me to tap that wet pussy of yours. You better be happy you don't have time right now. My beard misses bathing in your sweetness." Deshawn said as he pulled me closer, allowing me to feel his imprint protruding through his jeans. I was turned on and instantly felt my essence preparing for his tongue lashing.

"DeShawn, I can't baby. I have to get ready. I have ten minutes before my meeting starts."

"I know." He said as his hands made their way up my dress. He slid his fingers between my thighs. Knowing that I don't wear panties because I don't like panties lines. Deshawn's fingers rushed deep into my hotspot. And just like that I showered his digits with a rainfall of sweetness. I moaned softly as he stroked me. DeShawn pulled away, leaving me wanting more. I watched as he sucked his fingers clean. He then kissed me long and hard, allowing me to taste my essence.

"I'll let you get back to work. I hope I can finish what we started later tonight. You'll fill me in on all the details of the presentation?"

I just shook my head yes, as Deshawn exited my office. I was trying to catch my breath as the sound of Tamika buzzing me snapped me out of my daze.

"What now Tamika!" I snapped.

"Well, it's not another man with flowers," she joked. "Everyone is gathered in the conference room. They are ready. Good luck"

"Thank you, Tamika."

I gathered myself by fixing my clothes. Focus, I warned. You got this. I walked out of my office and down the hallway into the conference room. If only I was this confident in my love life as I am about this presentation, maybe I wouldn't have agreed to see DeShawn and Radir tonight. Lord, help me. Make these people see the vision I created and for me to get my shit together. Who was I fooling? God didn't do confusion. That shit was all on me.

CHAPTER TWENTY

I had managed to keep dinner with Radir to just dinner. He was disappointed, but I didn't care. He was like a dangerous drug that I desperately needed to rehabilitate myself from. Again. After the close call in my office with both him and DeShawn surprising me, I really need to get my shit together. I was feeling horrible about what I was doing to DeShawn. I had never been the cheating type. As many times as my heart had been broken by the weak actions of others, I never wanted to be the source of such pain. Deshawn was the first man to truly love me. All of me. I couldn't keep doing this to him. It was unfair. Especially when you consider who I was doing the cheating with.

I had made up my mind to end things with Radir at dinner. Every time I attempted to bring up the subject with him, he started talking about me and our future together. It was like he completely forgot that I was already with someone. Or maybe he just didn't care. He was voicing all the things I wanted to hear seven years ago. All the things I had dreamed of. A future as his wife, living the American Dream in luxury with a powerful husband by my side and me climbing the corporate ladder. The dream team and couple's goals that I had watched play out on my

Facebook timeline or Instagram for you page. I wanted that badly. I used to want that with Radir.

"Radir, why say all these things to me now? I waited for you. There wasn't anything I wouldn't do for you, and you broke my heart," I stated calmly as the tears rushed down my face. I couldn't hold back the pain I felt from the excitement in his words.

Radir left his seat and kneeled beside me. He took my hand in his. There was a pause before he spoke. "Evette, I wasn't ready for what you were willing to offer me back then. I was young and dumb. I didn't realize what I had in front of me when I had you. I was too stuck on superficial shit. I allowed other people to dictate to me what was right for me. I should have listened to my heart. I've always loved you. I guess I never stopped. I see that ring on your finger. But you're not married yet, which means there is still a chance I can win you back. All I ask is you give me a chance. Evette. Can you do that? Will you do it for us?"

"I need time to sort all this out, Radir," I said as I excused myself from the table and went to the restroom. I returned with my face erased of any tear stains and my lipstick freshened. To my surprise, there was a guy seated at the table with Radir. I walked up to the table, interrupting their conversation.

"Cameron, this is my lady, Evette. Evette, this is Cameron or Cam, as we call him." Radir introduced us.

Cam didn't look like someone that worked with Radir. His street attire, while high fashion, definitely read money, but not the kind you make in the office building. "Hello Cameron. Nice to meet you." I spoke, ignoring the label Radir placed on our situation.

"Damn Ray, I see you nigga, She thick as hell," Cam stated as he looked me over. I took my seat and glared at Radir.

"Excuse me Evette." Radir said.

"Yea, it was nice to meet you, Evette. Hopefully, I'll see you again," Cam said as he and Radir walked away from the table. I finished my dessert that awaited me. Radir finally reemerged. I had so many questions but decided to focus on the immediate issues. After the flood that flowed down my face, I refused to allow myself to be victim to another public display of emotional instability. I ended the night. I wouldn't even allow Radir to walk me to my car for fear that it would lead to something more.

When I arrived home, I wanted nothing more than to wash the stress of the day off me. It was still early. The time on my cellphone read seven. The next text was from DeShawn.

> **DeShawn-**
> I'm on my way. See You soon.

With everything that happen today, I really didn't want to be bothered. But I knew turning DeShawn away wasn't an option. After all, he was my fiancé; even though I hadn't been the most loving fiancé to him. I gathered my thoughts and got myself together. I went into my closet and put on the sexiest lingerie that I had. It was one of the outfits that DeShawn had picked out for me when we visited the boutique downtown. The silk and lace felt so good on my skin. I sprayed Killian's Good Girl Gone Bad everywhere I wanted Deshawn to kiss. My skin glistened from the shimmer body oil I ordered off of IG and my strappy Jimmy

Choo's adorned my feet. I put on the matching sheer robe, tossed my hair and freshened up my makeup just as the doorbell rang.

I walked with confidence through my condo and answered the door. There in front of me stood Deshawn. He was wearing a tailored black suit. He was carrying the biggest bouquet of red roses and a bottle of black label champagne. He was the most handsome man I had set eyes on.

"Damn E!" He said as his eyes gazed over my ensemble. The admiration in his eyes and the sinister grin that followed told me that he liked what he saw. Deshawn walked in and placed the flowers and champagne on the table in the foyer. He wrapped his arms around me and kissed me like we hadn't seen each other in days. The reality was it had only been hours. But from the embrace, he had been thinking about me since the last time we saw each other. Our lips parted just long enough for me to whisper, "You look handsome"

"This old suit," he joked.

"And you smell even better," I whispered as I sucked on his neck. His soft moans were all the motivation I needed to continue. The way his hands glided over the delicate fabric sent warm sensations up and down my body. There wasn't much to say other than "Fuck me Daddy" and with that, DeShawn came out of his suit. First the jacket, the popping sounds of his buttons falling off as I aggressively removed the custom shirt off of him, exposing his chiseled body. I kissed his chest and licked over his nipples, tracing his tattoos with my tongue. His hands ran through my tossed tresses as my hands unbuckled his belt and unzipped his pants, causing them to fall to the floor.

DeShawn picked me up with ease and backed me up against the living room window. His massive hands cuffed my ass as he squeezed, causing me to moan. I could feel his protruding manhood knocking on the silk material, begging to enter me. I reached down and moved the delicate material to the side and allowed DeShawn to enter me. His stiff rod caused my back to arch and a slow gasp escaped me as I took all of him in. With one hand Deshawn held onto me as the other hand cupped my full-size breast. The way he sucked and tugged on my nipples drove me crazy. I held on tight with my legs securely wrapped around his waist and arms draped around his neck.

With each thrust, his electrifying dick sent me into shock. I wondered how I could ever be unfaithful to someone like this. The way DeShawn laid the pipe was nothing short of being a god and here I was acting like a heathen. He stroked me with such care and force that my sanctuary exploded with excitement all over his stiffness. I saw a smile creep across his face as I released repeatedly. Our steady, heavy breathing and the slapping sound of our bodies was the only music filling the house. There we were, untamed against the streetlights and city skyline mirrored through the glass wall of windows that showcased our animalistic lovemaking. And just when I thought I couldn't give him any more of my juices, Deshawn turned me around. With my breast planted against the window, created new sensations for me to water his hard dick with.

That was just round one of the evening. Deshawn loved every inch of my body all over the condo. And just when I thought we were done, he dicked me down even more. If it wasn't his tongue game causing me to leak hot cream on his beard, his erections kept me cumming. By the time we were done, it was three in the morning. Thank God it was Friday. DeShawn had sweated my hair out. And with all we had done, I still craved him. I laid next to him as we ate on the chocolate-covered strawberries, and I filled him in on my presentation details. I could feel my insides yearning for him.

"Baby, I am so proud of you. So, what does this mean for your career?"

"Well, I'm certainly up for Senior Partner. Oh, and a raise."

"That's what's up. My Baby Bossed up. How lucky I am to have you in my life"

" What do you mean by that?"

"Mean by what?"

"Lucky to be with a Boss Chick?"

"I mean just what I said. I'm fortunate to have you in my life. You're the best thing to happen to me."

"You mean me or my money?"

"Yo, what are you talking about? Why would you say something like that to me?" DeShawn sat up and unraveled his arm from around me.

"I' just saying. I'll be the breadwinner in this relationship. Your job can't compare to my career. Of course, being with me is a step up."

"Wow. Is that what you think? That I care about your pockets?"

"DeShawn, you're a trash collector, a sanitation worker with no college education and a felony record."

"Ok. So, I can only be with you because you have money. Or what you can do for me? Is that what you really think?"

That's not what I said. I'm just saying, the promotion puts me in a different tax bracket. I'll be the breadwinner."

"The breadwinner. The executive that's married to the garbage man. Is that a problem for you Evette?" There was an awkward pause. Then DeShawn got up.

"Where are you going?"

"I need some air."

"So, you're just going to leave?" I said as I attempted to grab DeShawn's hand before he snatched away from me. "DeShawn!"

"DeShawn what?! What do you want from me, Evette? I'm a decent man making an honest living. Not once have I ever asked you for shit! I'm sitting here wanting to give you the world, and you don't think I'm good enough for you."

"That's not it DeShawn!"

"Then what is it? What the fuck is it? I'm good enough to fuck your brains out, but not good enough to do much else? DeShawn stated as he grabbed a pair of sweatpants out of the closet.

"DeShawn, wait!" I called after him as he left the bedroom.

I followed behind him as my naked body exposed my insecurities. "DeShawn!" I called after him, but he was already gone. I heard the front door slam behind him. I stood there wondering how I allowed myself to push away the only man who loved what so many couldn't. The tears once again flowed down my face. This time, instead of staining my face, the streams of tears penetrated my heart. It burned like nothing I had experienced before with DeShawn.

CHAPTER TWENTY-ONE

I drove around that night, just allowing the air to calm me down. It was too late to go get a drink and since the pandemic, most stores closed early. Although I didn't want to return home, I couldn't stay with Evette right now. I had to walk away before we both said something we would regret. I just needed a few moments to clear my head. Maybe my boys were right. I should have told Evette about my money. But my experiences with women told me most only wanted me for my reputation and the money they thought I had. I ain't never been a nigga tricking on females. But maybe that conversation with her was well overdue. It could have prevented what happened tonight. I mean, I certainly didn't want Evette thinking she needed to take care of me. That would never be the case. I was neva that kind of dude.

The night air had done what I needed it to do. After an hour and a half of aimlessly driving around, I was parked right next to Evette's car. I sat there for another hour before heading back upstairs. I turned the keys and doorknob slowly. I didn't want to wake Evette up. To my surprise, she was already up. She was sitting in the living room as the sun rise slowly crept across the sky. She was wrapped I a throw blanket and I could tell that she had been crying. Something I never wanted to be the cause of.

"You've been crying" I asked.

"Yes."

"Look Evett.."

"No DeShawn. I'm so sorry. I never meant to imply that you were not good enough for me. You are everything I want and need. It was just the stress of everything and just thinking about making sure we're going to be financially stable. I didn't mean to upset you," she said with a sheepish demeanor.

"Baby, we will be. I been meaning to tell you something."

"Can it wait DeShawn. I'm just happy you're back," she stated as she walked over toward me, allowing the throw to fall by the waist side. Evette dropped low, tugging at my sweatpants. She removed my member and slowly slid him into her warm mouth. Her gentle strokes and the twisting of her tongue as she guided me in and out of her was all the apology I needed. I watched as she worked me into a full erection. The way she worked her hands and mouth simultaneously made me wanna burst. I rocked back and forth as she took me deep down her throat. It wasn't until she murmured, "Come for me, Daddy" that the instant stream of thick liquid coated her throat. I watched as she swallowed and, without hesitation, took me back into her mouth and worked me up again.

I made us breakfast before we took a midmorning nap. By the time we woke up, it was dinnertime. We both got dressed, and I took Evette out to celebrate her. Not just the presentation, but because I truly was lucky to have her in my life. I had never known a woman like her. She had every right to want the finer things in life. She was accustomed to living a certain lifestyle that she earned all on her own. The fact that I could match that energy and lifestyle was a plus. In time she would know just how perfect we really were for each other. Evette didn't want to rehash the finance conversation right now but promised that we would sit down and discuss everything. Right now, she just wanted to spend quality time with me, and I was ok with that.

CHAPTER TWENTY-TWO

"Bitch, where have you been?" CeCe asked.

"Yea, Gurrl?!" Bridgette asked.

"Well, if you must know, I've been busy working. Y'all know I had that big presentation."

"And..." Sharmaine said excitedly.

"Bitch, you know I killed it. They just told me today I have the account!" I screamed out loud, causing the other patrons of the restaurant to look at us.

"Waitress, we're going to need a bottle of your best champagne" Sharmaine order by waving over our waitress.

"Is that all you been up to?"

"Girl, that was enough." I tried to exit the conversation, but I knew exactly what Sharmaine was hinting towards.

"I'm sure it was. I'm so happy for you. Senior VP of Marketing, here you come," CeCe said, raising her half empty glass in the air. The rest of the girls followed suit.

"So, how's DeShawn and the wedding plans coming along?" Bridgette asked.

"I haven't had time for any actual planning. Hopefully now that this project is over, I can put all my energy into wedding planning."

"Won't that be hard to do with Radir still in the picture?" Sharmaine said it in an evil, twisted way. She was the only person I had shared any recent revelations with about my situation with him. I gave her the side eye as if to sarcastically say "thanks, bitch."

"Evette, I just know you're not still entertaining Radir?" CeCe scoffed.

"Yeah. With everything that has happened between you two, shouldn't he be left in the past where he belongs?" Bridgett said.

"Y'all already know that nigga got in her panties and is making himself at home," Sharmaine joked.

"What about DeShawn? Evette, that man loves you." CeCe stated.

"I know. I planned on telling Radir it was over but.."

"But what? You don't owe him anything? Drop that nigga before DeShawn finds out and you lose everything." CeCe warned.

"Don't listen to them. If you wanna play the field, why not? You're not married yet," Sharmaine chimed in.

"Don't listen to her. She ain't been in a genuine relationship since junior high."

"And I won't because these men ain't shit!"

"Seriously Evette. Don't play the same game that had you messed up for years. DeShawn deserves better. You deserve better," Bridgette cautioned.

"I know. DeShawn means the world to me."

"If he meant the world to you, you wouldn't be tagging Radir. Leave that garbage man alone and get yours," Sharmaine laughed.

The rest of the girls looked on in disgust. I hated that she brought up my indiscretions. I shared those things with her in confidence. "Listen ladies, my personal life is not up for discussion. Can we drop it, please?" I sang out, annoyed.

"Fine." Sharmaine commented. Everyone else wore their sentiments on their faces. We finished up dinner and drinks, but the vibe of the evening was lost. I never wanted my sex life to be on display. I knew I was wrong for cheating on DeShawn. Worse, I had no way of fixing this situation I created. Radir was relentless in his quest to win me back. I was finally hearing him admit that I was the woman he wanted to be with. My mind told me to run far away from Radir because he had his chance at loving me and failed miserably. DeShawn loved me. But my heart sang a different song. I guess I was never really over Radir. It was the only way to explain the hold he still had on me and my body.

A few days had passed since I met up with my girls. Bridget had stopped by my place for drinks after work. She wanted to share with me some ideas for the bridal shower. I had just enough time to make it home and change before the doorbell rang. I looked at my phone and the notification from the Ring Camera told me that Bridgette had arrived.

"Hey girl," I said as I opened the door. Bridgette was carrying a bag of goodies and an armful of magazines.

"Hey lady. Thanks for having me over."

"Is it just you and I tonight?"

"Yeah. I hope you don't mind. I wanted to talk to you without all the drama some of the other ladies bring." She said with a charming smile.

"Oh, you mean to tell me Sharmaine won't be joining us," I sarcastically grinned.

"Yeah, the other day was a mess."

"Huh!" I rolled my eyes as the conversation from the other day replayed in my mind at hyper speed.

"Girl, I brought by some of the desert table goodies in the color theme of your wedding. There is also a bottle of Rosé I want you to try. It is one of my favorite new wines. I thought we could start coming up with a plan for what you would like for the bridal party to do for your shower. Bridgette stated as she unpacked the cloth bag full of treats.

We sat at the countertop bar in the kitchen tastings and examining the treats until we finally narrowed the array of fifteen items down to eight items that would be featured on the bridal party sweets table, moving on to the decorations, centerpieces, and finally flowers. By the time we finished up, Bridgette had a well-rounded idea of what I wanted. We narrowed down the list of party planners to two young ladies whose reputation was stellar. She would be taking the lead on the bridal shower and would rally the rest of the bridal party around my vision.

"Thank you, Bridgette. This was actually fun."

"Girl, you don't have to thank me. That's what friends do."

"I know but with all I have had going on.. well, let's just say planning the wedding hasn't been a priority."

" Wait, you're not thinking of calling it off? You want to marry DeShawn? Right?"

"Of course I want to get married."

"As a trash collector! You yourself reminded me of that. Hell, you all reminded me of that and his felonious past. I have an opportunity to be happy. Why can't you see that"

" Evette, I thought you were happy. I thought DeShawn makes you happy. We just spent three hours planning a wedding. Who the fuck are you planning on marrying, because right now I don't know, and it sounds like you don't know either."

"You have no right to come at me like that. I have supported every poor decision you have ever made. No Judgement. I know that this is fucked up. I don't need you, Sharmaine, or the rest of you to remind me.

"Listen, I'm not judging you. I just think you deserve to be happy. But I can't stand by and watch you make this mistake. DeShawn deserves better and so do you."

Just then the door opened. DeShawn was home. In all our excitement I lost track of time and forgot that he would be home soon. He walked into an awkward silence. I'm sure he felt the tension in the room as Bridgette and I stood there like deer caught in the headlights.

"Is everything ok ladies?" DeShawn quizzed.

"Yeah," Bridgette chuckled as she gathered her things up.

"Hey baby. Bridgette and I were in the middle of a heated conversation about the wedding. You know how intense we can get," I jokingly tried to convince DeShawn that was all there was to our heated debate. I wasn't sure if he bought it. He kissed my cheek and smiled.

"Hey Bridgette. I haven't seen you in a minute. How you doing?"

"I'm fine DeShawn. Just trying to knock some sense into your girl's head. But other than that, I'm good.

"That's not what I asked you. Do you want to marry DeShawn?"

There was a slight pause in my attempt to answer Bridgette.

"Girl, listen. I know I haven't been as supportive of your relationship with DeShawn as I should have been. But Evette, that man loves you. I see it. Hell, I feel it. The way he looks at you. The way he treats you. Not once has he ever said anything bad about you. Not to mention he is fine. What more could you ask for?"

"I don't know. I'm caught up in this horrible what-if scenario between DeShawn and Radir. In my mind I should be with DeShawn but my heart.. it wants..."

"Bitch, you better not say his name again. I just know you haven't allowed that snake to hook his poisonous fangs that deep into you. Evette, do you remember everything he put you through? The weeks of depression. The arguments. His controlling ways. For crying out loud, you cannot be serious!"

"I know. I know. But things are different now."

"Different how? Oh, let me tell you. Your confidence is back. You finally found someone who loves you. All of you. You have someone who is not intimidated by your curves, your education and career. He waits until your life is damn near, perfect to sliver back into your life and you let him."

"Bridgette, you don't know. Radir has changed. Plus, he and I can be the power couple I always dreamed of. DeShawn... He can't give me that, at least not the way I need him to."

"So now you're superficial? DeShawn makes an honest living Evette."

"Well, don't hit her too hard. I need her to have all her faculties when she says yes to being my wife." DeShawn laughed as he hit me on my ass and walked out of the room, headed toward the bedroom. "I'm going to jump in the shower. I see you later Bridgette." He yelled as he closed the door behind him.

"I'm going to head out." Bridgette said as she dropped the pleasantries that were on display for DeShawn.

"Bridgette.." I attempted to stop her from leaving like this. But she was gone before I could even finish my sentence.

CHAPTER TWENTY-THREE

"Man, maybe she just tired of yo ass!" Mike laughed.
"Nah dog that ain't it" I laughed back.
"No seriously, maybe you just need to step up the romance game a little bit. I know when Shareece is acting up, it's usually time for us to get away. Bruh, you need to plan a getaway for you and Evette. I bet after a week or weekend away things will be ok."

"You're right, Greg. It's been a while since we took a vacation. Evette has been so busy with work even our weekend baecations have taken a back seat. Maybe it's time I took my baby away."

"So, where are you thinking?"

"I'm not sure. I'm going to have to do some homework and figure out her schedule. Last thing I wanna do is plan a trip, and she has to work."

The fellas and I continued our conversation. They gave me a few more suggestions and things to do. They wouldn't be my boys if it didn't come with side jokes and jabs at my expense. It was all good. Sense I didn't have any biological brothers, Mike,

Greg and a few of my other friends had stepped into the role for me. We were tight like that and I respected their opinion. Didn't say I would always abide by their suggestions. Hell, half the shit that came out of their mouths was dumb as hell. It explained why half of them were still single at their age. But I knew they had my back and respected my relationship with Evette. They were pulling for us just as much as I was.

Evette just didn't seem to act like her normal self. With her presentation over, I assumed her workload wouldn't be as stressful. That she could concentrate on us a little more. The only thing that was back to normal was me spending time at her place more. Even with me being back, she seemed distracted. There were nights when we would watch television and she didn't seem interested, even though it was one of her favorite shows. Or when I cooked dinner and wanted to talk about our day, her responses were terse and lacked the enthusiasm I had become accustomed to. I was sure that planning a romantic getaway would do us both some good.

I called Evette's office. When Tamika answered the phone, I was happy to hear her voice. She was the one person I knew who could help me pull off my surprise vacation. Her sassy street vibes were a welcome tone, considering that she worked in a corporate environment.

"Banks, Lewis and Hough Marketing Firm. You have reached the office of Evette Watts. How may I assist you?"

"Hey Tamika. This is DeShawn."

"Hey, handsome. Evette is in a meeting right now. Would you like her voice mail?"

"No. I actually need to speak with you."

"Really?" Tamika spoke with excitement in her voice. "Well, what can I help you with?"

"I'm trying to surprise Evette with a romantic vacation. I can't do that unless I know what her schedule looks like. Is there any dates you can suggest? I mean, I really wanna do something nice for her. Can you help me?"

"Say less! I know our girl has been hella busy lately keeping those late office hours. But I can make sure that she has time for this. Let me see what I can do. I gotchu!"

"Thanks Tamika. I appreciate this."

"I wish a man would plan a romantic anything for me. I don't know if Evette knows how good she got it." Tamika commented.

"I'm sure she does. Thanks again for your help. Take down my number so you can call me if you need to."

"Trust me I have your number already. I'll be in touch."

With Tamika assisting me with planning the surprise getaway, I decided to enlist Evette's girls with helping me plan a surprise bridal shower. I know that Evette and Bridgette had come up with some ideas, but maybe I can help bring all those ideas to life. I asked Bridgett and CeCe to meet me for coffee on Saturday. They both agreed. I asked them to bring any ideas on the bridal shower with them. I could tell there was some hesitance but once I explained what I wanted to do, they both were on board. As soon as I hung up the phone, I called the florist and had them deliver three dozen white roses to Evette's condo. If romance was what we needed, I was more than prepared to get us back on track.

I made my way back to Evette's place. I started thinking about life after we were married. All this back and forth between my place and her place had me thinking it was time for us to find our place. Something we both could invest in and make a home. I didn't have a problem with the condo life. Evette just made it clear when we started dating that this was "her place". I was welcome to spend the night and keep a few items at her place, but it never felt like a place I could truly call home. It didn't matter to me because I had a home of my own. But if we were going to be husband and wife it was time we looked for a place of our own. A place we could mutually coexist in.

While I waiting I ordered some groceries to be delivered and cleared out the shopping carts that were open on Evette's tablet. This was something I did from time to time. Evette would complain sometimes about me doing that. But I felt like there was no need to ever wait for something you want. If she added it to the cart then it was worth purchasing. Besides, any woman that I was with didn't need to wait on anything. That was what I was here for. To make sure she knew she could count on me to notice the big and the small details about her.

The groceries were delivered. I immediately started preparing dinner. I was in the middle of seasoning the salmon fillets with my homemade blacked seasoning when the doorbell rang. Evette wasn't home yet. She told me she would be home late tonight, so I wasn't expecting anyone other than the florist with my order of flowers.

I opened the door and there stood an unfamiliar face.
"Hey, Wuzup?"
"My bad, I think I have the wrong floor."

"No problem. I felt like that too when I first started coming here."

"Thanks"

I watched as the stranger in the well-tailored suite walked down the hallway. Just as he disappeared, I saw the delivery guy holding the three dozen white roses I ordered. He carefully made his way to the door. I tipped him and closed the door behind him. I went back to cooking.

Evette arrived home just as I was finishing up dinner. I instructed her to get comfortable as I plated the blackened honey glazed salmon, saffron rice and asparagus. We ate at the countertop and enjoyed dinner and small talk over a sweet California wine. I could tell that something was weighing heavily on her mind.

"Evette, is everything ok?" My question seemed to catch her off guard.

"Yea. I'm just tired."

"Baby, I hate to see you working yourself like this. Is there anything I can do to help you relax?"

"No. You do enough. I appreciate you so much." I turned to face her. There was an innocence to her. I could tell that she meant the words she spoke. But something was bothering her. I let it go. When she was ready to open up to me, I believed she would. For now, her words would be enough.

"Come here, baby". I said, pulling her towards me. I held her tightly. I felt our breathing sync and a calmness cover her. I released her from my grip. Maybe too early as she sighed, letting me know she wanted more.

"Don't let me go," she whispered.

I picked her up into my arms and carried her over to the couch in the living room. We cuddled in the still of the evening. We sat there in silence as Evette rested in my embrace. It was the best way to end the work week.

CHAPTER TWENTY-FOUR

"Radir make this quick. I am supposed to be home packing," I said as I marched into the hotel room. No sooner had the words left my mouth, Radir appeared. His sculpted body was draped in a pristine white terry cloth towel. It hung right around his waist, showing off just enough of his muscular v that pointed to my kryptonite. His body was covered in droplets of water and the devious grin made my loins ach with excitement.

"Hey baby," he said pulling me in close to him.

"Nah. I'm not here for this" I said shaking my head and trying hard to convince myself that I didn't want what he was about to offer me.

"What I do?

"Nothing. I told you we were over."

"But I know you didn't mean it."

"Radir, I meant every word that I said to you. I'm engaged to someone who loves me. All of me. I can't do this anymore with you." He just stood there looking me over. I could feel the hunger through his stares. I don't know why this man made me so goddamn nervous.

"You don't even mean that shit now and you didn't mean it then. I know you want me just as much as I want you. I know you Evette, better than you know yourself. I know you think about me. I know you want someone who compliments you in all the right ways. I know you need someone that can keep you living the lifestyle you're accustomed to. I can do that and more. That's why you came. Because you know it too." Radir said as she slowly circled me. My heartbeat became erratic and my breathing heavy with anticipation. He was right, but that was not what was best for me. Deshawn was my future, I attempted to convince myself as Radir planted his warm lips on the nape of my neck.

I tried to push away from his embrace, but my legs were paralyzed. My heart had betrayed me without warning. Radir's body pressed against me as I melted into him. "I can't" I whispered.

"But I can for the both of us" he whispered in my ear.

I woke up wrapped in Radir's arms. It was three in the morning.

"Fuck" I yelled out loud. I scurried around the room gathering my clothes and rushing to get dressed.

"What are you doing?"

"I got to go. I can't.." I said as I slipped my shoes on and hurried out of the room. I fingered my hair in the elevator mirrored walls. Finally, I reached the ground floor. I quickly made my way to my car. It wasn't until I was safely seated in my vehicle that I took a moment to breathe. The tears slowly started to roll down my face. I was losing my grip on this situation. I wasn't sure how much longer I could keep this up. I was playing a serious game of chess like I was an expert in checkers. There was no way I could win. I was setting myself up to fail at love again if I kept this up. I was too damn old to be running out of hotel rooms and sneaking around. "Damnit Evette! Get your shit together girl!" I yelled at myself as I put the car in reverse, backing out of the parking space and proceeded to drive out of the parking garage.

I made it home. The only good thing about tonight was that DeShawn was out of town. He had a family emergency in Buffalo he needed to attend to. He was vague about whatever was going on. He left early yesterday morning. I dropped him off at the airport. If it hadn't been for that, his ass would have been at my place waiting for me. I would have been busted coming in at this ungodly hour of the morning. It was too late to do anything other than shower and finish packing. I had a client meeting today. They were flying me out on their private jet. I was given an itinerary and the ledger said to pack for the tropics. They were sending a car to pick me up at five-thirty.

The doorman buzzed me to let me know the car service was here to pick me up. I told him I would be right there. I locked up the condo and made my way to the front lobby of my building. The driver quickly grabbed my bags and placed them in the trunk of the all-black sedan. When the driver was done, he opened the passenger side back door for me. The stout older gentleman closed the door behind me and in silence drove me to the air pad where the private jet was waiting. The only thing Tamika, my assistant, told me was that the client was very adamant about disclosing any information on the brand and the project they were hiring me for.

According to the itinerary, the only details provided were the date and time of the flight. I was instructed to pack for tropical weather and to turn my cell phone in to the security team once I arrived at my destination. I figured this must be a very high-profile company. I was more than willing to have the conversation and to get away for a few days to clear my hand.

The jet landed. I must have nodded off during the trip. Somewhere between my French style breakfast and coffee, I must have drifted off to sleep. After the night I had I was amazed that I even made the flight. I heard the captain announce that we had arrived and would be descending into the beautiful island of Antigua. My mind immediately went to Rihanna and her Fenty Cosmetic line. What an opportunity if this was true! Why else would I be in the Caribbean? I mean, what company flies a prospective marketing agent to a tropical island for a work meeting unless the CEO is native to the islands? My heart raced with excitement and then panic.

I quickly grabbed my purse and looked at my face in my compact mirror. "Oh Shit!" I need to fix my face. I cannot get off this aircraft looking like I just got up. There was no way Rihanna or her team at Fenty would ever take me seriously looking like this. I immediately sprayed my face with a priming mist, followed by a tinted moisturizer. I used my sun kissed lip gloss and dabbed my eye lids with it. It gave my eye lids a slight spark and youthful appearance. Finally, I did a quick cat eye mascara line on both eyes and glossed my lips with the same color I used on my eye lids. I finger combed my hair and just as the doors to the cabin of the jet opened, I was ready.

CHAPTER TWENTY-FIVE

Thanks to Tamika's clever antics, I could plan an amazing get-a-way to Antigua for Evette. Everything was perfectly planned. The only thing Evette would know was that a prospective client wanted to meet with her. This was the only way to get Evette out of the office and to surprise her. Allowing her to think she was meeting with a prospective client was a sure way that she would show up uninterrupted. So, when the hotel staff picked her up and requested her cell phone to abide by the client's confidentiality clause, she was more than willing to hand it over. I wanted to make sure that I limited any distractions that could come from having Evette tethered to her phone.

The all-inclusive resort was breathtakingly beautiful. It offered a panoramic view of the island from every angle of the compound. The temperature was a tropical ninety-one degrees. The resort staff all wore white linen clothing to help to stay cool while working. Their attire also made for a polished, cohesive professional look. I had followed suit and took hints from the few staff members I came in contact with. I wore all cotton blend clothing and even purchased a couple of short sets from a nearby upscale clothing boutique. I didn't pack enough comfortable clothing options for the trip. Nothing could have prepared me for the temperature and the constant beaming sun's rays. I wasn't sure what to expect with traveling internationally. I am still new to passport travel. When you have a felonious past, there are many hoops you have to jump through to get a passport. I'm still wondering how the hell they approved my application. This was only my second internal vacation. My first trip when I got out of prison was to Cancun. Fortunately, I didn't need a passport for that trip.

Evette and I had taken small trips around the country together. A weekend or holiday get-a-way here and there. She was the one who encouraged me to get my passport. Everything I had been told that felons didn't qualify was not true. I had to do some pleading and even went before the court. After gathering a few signatures and extra documentation and waiting six months, my request for a passport was granted. Evette and I had plans to travel more often, but her work schedule always got in the way. Not that I am complaining, hell I was ready whenever the opportunity turned up. And since things at home had been off with me and Evette, the opportunity was now. I just hated tricking her like this.

The door to the bungalow opened and, to Evette's surprise, I was standing there in the center of the room with the glass floor underneath my feet showing off the clear blue water of the island.

"DeShawn, what is going on?"

"Hey, baby. Surprise," I said as I walked over to greet her. I handed her the bouquet of peach roses and gardenias that I picked especially for her arrival. I lunged in to kiss her, and she backed away.

"Deshawn, what is going on? I am here to meet a prospective client. Why are you here?"

"Yeah, about that. I'm your client. I mean.. well, I wanted to surprise you with a vacation. Some time for the two of us to reconnect and just relax. You've been so busy with work and projects that I thought you could use some time away from the office. Tamika was kind enough to help me plan this trip for you. I hope you're not angry."

"You did what! How dare you? And you involved my assistant?" The tone in her voice told me she was not happy.

"Look Evette. You're here now. You and I are together. Let's just enjoy the view and our time at the resort." I slyly whispered as I wrapped my arms around her curves. Slowly, Evette's frown gave way to a half smile as she glanced over the bungalow and took in the scenery.

"You did this for me?"

"Yes. I did this for us, baby."

"But how can you...?"

"I will tell you everything you need to know. But first. I pulled Evette into me and kissed her soft lips. The mere scent of her perfume and the touch of her hands around my neck sent my body into shock. My member jumped in my linen shorts and instantly hardened as Evette's body pressed against mine. I undressed Evette right where she stood. She allowed my tongue to caress her body as she moaned softly. I found my way to the center of her flower as my beard tickled her inner thighs. I sucked her stigma until she blessed me with her nectar. It was two in the afternoon, and I was happy to say our vacation was off to a great start.

At first, Evette was hesitant to relax. Thank God I had them take her cell phone away when she arrived. And with limited internet coverage, Evette had to enjoy herself away from work. We set out each day to conquer the island. We did everything from snorkeling, sightseeing, shopping, eating the local cuisine to dancing the night away at the resort hosted night club. Evette had finally let her hair down. I was seeing the woman I loved and remembered resurfacing.

"You look beautiful,"
"Thank you, baby. Just a little sumthin' sumthin' my man brought me."
"Oh, so you have a man?" I laughed.
Evette's demeanor instantly changed at the sound of my joke.
"What is that supposed to mean?"
"Hold up, I was just joking, ma. What's with the attitude?"
I saw Evette take a few deep breaths. "Are you ok?" I asked.
"Yeah, I'm ok. I'm sorry for the outburst. I think all this time in the sun may have gotten to me. I'm sure the endless cocktails I've been drinking are not helping either."
"Baby, I just need you to relax a little. That's what this escape is all about. We have a week to lie back and enjoy ourselves." I commented as I walked towards her and embraced her into my arms. Her tense muscles relaxed just enough for her to lean back into me. "I gotchu baby." I whispered as the image of orange and red tones cascaded across the sky as the setting sun came to rest.

Dinner was amazing. I felt like I had finally gotten through to Evette. She seemed to live in the moment with me. I wasn't sure why she was so on edge but being engulfed by the beauty of the island and the magic of being surrounded by melanated people did something to me. I hoped it was having the same influence on Evette. After dinner, we headed over to a nightclub that was on the resort property. We danced and allowed the drinks to flow. Our bodies intertwined as if we were native islanders. The rhythm was hypnotic and sensual. After all that rubbing up against each other, it wasn't long before the urge to take Evette and have my way with her presented itself with the bulging imprint of my manhood through the linen pants I was wearing. Evette noticed it as she kept backing her ass into me. Her wicked grin suggested she relished in the teasing all the grinding and ass shaking was doing to me.

"You keep that up and I will fuck you right here in front of everyone." I uttered through the sounds of the music. I knew she heard me, the surprised expression on her face said as much. She must've thought I wasn't a man of my word, so I grabbed her thick thighs as she pushed into me. The club lights were dim enough that the only thing you could see were the shadows of bodies colliding against each other. It looked like art, the way the images reenacted sexual movements and tones as the music guided their next move. Everyone was under their own spell. No one had time to worry about the next couple. So, when my hands made their way up Evette's thighs and into her moist garden, causing her mouth to open as she gasped for air, mimicked the sounds that flooded the club, no one paid her or me any attention.

I parted her interior lips with my index finger as her dress rode up on her hips from the way she threw her ass back onto me. She rested her upper body on me and I wrapped my arm around her waist, holding her captive to the beat of my fingers, playing her clit like an ancestorial instrument. Our Bodies rocked to the mystical tones that swept through the night. The heat, the sexual undertones, and the magic of the island clarified that this was what I wanted in life. Evette was the woman for me. I wanted to be with her whenever possible. If she would let me, I could care for her the way she deserved to be loved. I allowed my fingers to do all the talking as I strummed her until her internal rhythm caught up to my vibrations. She climaxed all over my fingers, causing my manhood to jump with the excitement of being next. Evette turned to look at me as she took my fingers into her mouth and licked her juices off of me. It was all the affirmation I needed. I scooped Evette up into my arms and carried her back to our bungalow.

The topical sounds swept through the isolated bungalow. There was nowhere to hide from the brightness of the early reflections of the sun. I laid in bed watching Evette sleep peacefully. I ordered breakfast for both of us. Evette may have had too much to drink and smoke last night. I got her some coffee and light food to help her feel better. Besides, I know dickin' her down the way I did had her resting strong. I got up and showered off the stickiness of last night's activities. It was almost noon, and I wanted to wake Evette, instead I opted to allow her to sleep in. I had a few things I wanted to do for her, so this gave me the opportunity to move about the island without her knowing all the surprises I had in store for her. I went to kiss her on her shoulder when I heard her whisper in her sleep, "Radir leave me alone."

Who the fuck was Radir?

CHAPTER TWENTY-SIX

"So, how was the trip?"
"Girl. I'm not sure how many checks DeShawn had to save up to afford that bungalow and the private jet to the island, but my man did that."

"No, he didn't!"

"Yass, he did! Not only that, but he showered me with all kinds of gifts. He planned the perfect vacation and spared no expense. Everything was first class. "I confessed, reminiscing about the past week.

"Well, I'm happy that your uptight ass had a relaxing baecation."

"I know, right? Girl, the things that man did to me are the stuff books are written about. Except..."

"Except what?" Brigette asked.

"Don't tell me you acted a fool?" Sharmaine questioned in an accusatory tone.

"No. At least I don't think I did anything."

"Evette, please tell me you weren't on your phone while DeShawn was trying to spend time with you."

I attempted to relive the week and searched for anything that could explain DeShawn's sudden change in behavior. But I came up with nothing. After I got over the initial shock of not meeting a client and set aside the drama with Radir, I could finally relax and appreciate everything DeShawn had done for me. "No, it's just that DeShawn started acting weird."

"Weird like what?"

"Hell, I didn't know felons could travel abroad, so him acting brand new doesn't surprise me," Sharmaine laughed.

"Fuck you Sharmaine. And for your information, DeShawn is more cultured than your hood ass." I laughed back at her.

"Then if that's not it, what do you mean?"

"I don't know. He just seemed off. The dick was amazing. The conversation flowed, and I thought we had a good time. He just seemed different from the second half of the trip. Maybe I'm just paranoid."

"Maybe this is the wake up call you needed." Bridgette slyly stated.

"What is that supposed to mean?"

"Girl, don't play dumb. That man loves you. Only you. Don't fuck that up."

She was right. But my love life was not hers. I knew DeShawn loved me. No one needed to remind me of that. But I wasn't married yet. Plus, I'm going to end things with Radir. At least that's what I should do. I think. Shit. Yes, I was going to end it with him. But I didn't need her or any of these heffas questioning me about it. "I know that. I'm not worried about DeShawn, and neither should you be. I can handle my man." I firmly stated as I rolled my eyes at the audacity of her statement. The room went silent. We all took a pause and drank a sip of the sweet California red wine that filled our stemless glasses.

"So, this wedding, are you ready?"

"Hell yeah. I know it's six months away. Time is going by so fast. I can't believe that I'm doing it. I'm so ready to be Mrs. Baugh." I proclaimed.

"Good. Keep that same energy, sis. The next couple of months will be hectic."

"Let's toast to getting this bitch down the aisle" Sharmaine joked. We all laughed as our glasses touched. I knew that getting married was everything I wanted. Ever since I was a little girl, I had dreamed of being someone's wife. No one ever said that my prince wouldn't be the man I wanted, but the man I needed. They would never be the same, and the thought of having one without the other made me sick to my stomach.

I waited up for DeShawn. It was unusual for him to arrive home later than me. With the new promotion at work, I could finally relax and delegate a lot of the minute stuff that used to take me away from spending time with DeShawn. Except, DeShawn hadn't been around as much since we returned home from our vacation. I even had to ask him to come over to my place, which was something he used to do without warning or invitation. When I asked him what was up, he just told me he had a lot on his mind and needed to take care of some family shit. It was just him and his sister, so I didn't know much of anything else that could go on in his family. Now that I think about it, I really didn't know much about DeShawn's family. I mean, I met everyone that counted according to him. We went to a few gatherings and occasionally over to his sister's house for special occasions, but nothing more than that. So, if there was something going on, I was out of the loop.

"Baby, is everything ok? " I asked. Deshawn had been very standoffish since we returned from Antigua. We were supposed to be watching this Tubi movie, but he didn't seem interested. He had been on his phone the entire time. I knew it wasn't work related. Hell, he was a sanitation worker. Wasn't no one texting him this late hour about picking up trash. I mean, I shouldn't say it like that, but it's the truth. It was pissing me off.

"I'm good."

"I can't tell. You seem preoccupied by something.

"It ain't nothing."

"It's something. Hell, you were on your phone the whole movie."

"I'm about to go lay down. I have to get up early tomorrow."

"Tomorrow is Saturday. You don't have to work." I attempted to communicate with him, but he stormed off, heading toward the bedroom. I don't have time for this shit. I just allowed him to walk away. The movie was almost over. Locking up the condo before heading to bed, I noticed my cellphone screen notification light up. Touching the screen, I saw a text from Radir.

Radir-
You Up?

Thank goodness I didn't open the message. I left the message on unread. Fuck that nigga too.

CHAPTER TWENTY-SEVEN

This is just what I needed I thought to myself. A good workout to blow off some steam always did me justice. This whole situation with Evette calling me some other nigga's name got me fucked up. Granted, she was sleeping. But I can't get over it. That shit rubbed me the wrong way. I took it out on the punching bag, hoping it would free me from the uneasy feeling that covered me. A few more reps and that should do it.

I finished up the full-body workout drenched in sweat. It felt good. It had been a long time since I got it in like that. My muscles were sure to be angry with me tomorrow. Wiping the sweat off my face and neck, I looked up to see the devil himself staring at me. This fool could not take a hint. Business in Grand Rapids must be bleak for this fool to keep coming down here bothering me. You would have thought that our last encounter would have been the last. Normally, families fight and make up. But we weren't brothers anymore. Not even close to being anything but former acquaintances. I grabbed my knapsack and water bottle as I finished wiping off the last piece of equipment I used before heading toward the door. I walked right past Cam and into the morning air.

"So, it's like that?"

I refused to engage him in a conversation. I kept walking toward my truck. I hit the key fob and loaded my things in the backseat. My intentions were to drive off and leave that fool right where he stood.

"Fine, I bet Evette will make time for me. You sure know how to pick them. Shorty thick and fine as hell. I mean, maybe she might let me in on the action." Cam laughed across the parking lot.

I slammed my car door. Without warning, all my frustrations of the past few weeks came hurling out of me as I approached Cam. Connecting my fist with his jaw, I yelled out, " Keep my girl's name out your mouth nigga." The force of my punch landed Cam on the asphalt. I wish I could say the punches stopped there. But they didn't. My hands kept connecting with him. It was just like when we were younger. Cam was not a fighter which was why he often opted for the gun. He would shoot a motherfucker with the quickness, but throwing hands was a last resort. A couple of guys in the gym ran out to pull me off of him. My hand was covered in blood, as was Cam's face.

He just laughed, spitting blood onto the pavement. "Your bitch ain't shit, nigga. I let you have this one. The next time, you won't be so lucky. You betta be glad you my brother,"

Yanking away from the three guys that held me back from finishing Cam off, I walked away from the scene.

"I know you hear me, Deshawn. Your bitch ain't shit, nigga.

I could hear his rant as I pulled off in a mad dash it get as far away from him as possible.

Instead of going back to Evette's crib, I went home. As soon as I hit the house, I went straight to the frig and popped open a cold beer. I grabbed the cold pack out of the freezer and placed it on my now swollen knuckles. I was pissed off. Not at Cam. He was just being his ignorant ass self. I was mad that this thing with Evette was getting the best of me. All that thinking for a change shit they taught me in prison went all out the window at the mention of her name coming from him. It was a class designed to help you manage your emotions and temper. It was a required course before any inmate could leave the facility. What they don't tell you is that mutherfuckas in the real world don't care about you and your feelings. Especially the ones that know they can push your buttons, something Cam knew how to do all too well with me.

I sat there at the kitchen island, nursing my hand and popping beer after beer. I didn't like feeling like this. The correct thing to do would be to just ask Evette, but why? I mean, she wouldn't. She couldn't. I thought to myself. Instantly I erased those thoughts from my head. Negro, get your shit together. I finished the last beer and headed to the bedroom to take a shower. I washed off Cam's blood and my anger from the morning. The hot water soothed my tension away. All except the echoing words of Cam's remark, "Your bitch ain't shit."

I dried off and wrapped the towel around my waist. Opening the first aid kit that I kept in the bathroom storage closet, I wrapped my hand in gauze and flexible tape before crawling into bed.

I woke up to several missed text and calls from Evette. I wanted to reply but decided that maybe I shouldn't until I fix my attitude. The last thing I wanted to do was go around in the ring with her. I might not lay hands on her, but I knew myself well enough to know my words could sting just as badly. There were a few other messages from Mike, Greg, and the crew inviting me to come out tonight. I quickly replied for them to save me a spot. I would be there in an hour. Maybe this is what I needed. A night out with my boys. I quickly pulled together an outfit, got dressed, and checked myself in the full-length mirror before heading out the door.

I pulled up to the lounge. There was a small crowd waiting in line to get in. You could hear the live band playing all the way in the parking lot as I stepped out of the truck. I walked up to the bouncers and dabbed them up. I knew Johnny and Big L from back in the day. They were shorties when I was running in the streets. To see them both all grown up and staying clean made my heart smile every time I saw them.

"What up bruh,"

"Shit, man."

"It's always good to see you dawg."

"Stay up, nephews," I said as they opened the door and signaled for me to enter.

Once inside the building, I saw familiar faces in the crowd. A few cover songs were played by the band, and the dance floor was packed. The energy was everything I was hoping for. The perfect distraction. First, I needed a drink in my hand. Something stronger than the Coors Light beers I guzzled down hours earlier. The petite bar stewardess smiled at me as she took my order.

"This is one is on the group of women at the end of the bar," she stated, pointing toward the ladies celebrating what appeared to be a bachelorette party. The sash and crown told me who the bride to be was in the crowd. I waved and smiled politely as they giggled. I turned around with the drink in my hand and surveyed the crowd. Spotting Greg and Mike at a corner table, I headed in that direction.

"What up player" I stated as I made my presence known.
"Oh shit! Look who made it outside."
Naw, don't do my man like that." Greg laughed.
"Fellas, I'm here." I smiled as we all laughed.
"Excuse me ladies, don't mind us. As you can see they don't have any manners. I'm Deshawn."

"Hey Deshawn, I'm Meeka. That's Cherelle and over there is Lisa," said the thin young lady in the red dress.

I took the seat in the corner facing the center of the club. I had a habit of never sitting with my back to the door. I needed to see who was coming and going, something that carried over with me from my time in the streets. Something as simple as where you sat caught a lot of dudes off guard. It could cost you your life and possibly your girl, depending on the situation. The young ladies were engaged in conversation. It was just like Mike and Greg to be entertaining some young honeys.

"So, Evette let you out tonight?"

"There you go with the jokes. Evette is not that the type to keep me on a leash like that. It just so happens that I enjoy spending time with my woman."

'Speaking of Evette, is she going to be joining us?"

"Naw. I'm solo tonight. Is that ok?"

"Yea, I'm just asking."

"Had I known y'all negroes were going to be coupled up, I would have invited her."

Mike and Greg laughed as they looked at the ladies at the table.

"Well, you know how we do."

"Everyone don't have a girl like Evette,"

I just smiled and sat back in the chair, nursing my drink. The band was good. This was my first time watching them. The lead vocalist had a sound that was reminiscent of Babyface Edmonds or John B. He was smooth and the female lead singer was hot. She had that Ashanti look with a powerful pair of lungs. As soon as the ladies at the table heard the start of the next song, they were up on their feet and headed to the dance floor, dragging Mike and Greg with them. I watched as Mike and Greg's old asses attempted to keep up with the young ladies dancing. It was comical. But not as silly as I looked sitting here alone. I started to take out my phone and text Evette. I was interrupted by the faint echo of someone calling my name.

"Deshawn." I heard the soft voice say through the music. It was so faint that I almost didn't hear it. "Deshawn." I looked in a different direction and noticed Bridgette heading in my direction.

"Hey B. What up doe?"

"What up D? Evette with you?"

"Naw, she at home. I'm out with my boys from work."

"Ok, I see you."

We both laughed.

"Who you here with?"

"My cousins from Detroit came over this way for the weekend. So here I am hanging with them crazy chicks."

"Where they at?" She pointed to the center of the dance floor. "Lisa, Meeka and Cherelle?" I said, laughing.

"Yup. How you know them?"

"Those are my boys they dancing with." We both took one more look at the group dancing in the middle of the floor and burst out laughing.

"Wow," I said shaking my head. The girls were throwing it back on Mike and Greg. Asses were twerking. Both Mike and Greg looked like they had no clue what to do with it. " And that's why you shouldn't be the old guy at the club." Bridgette and I had a good laugh at their expense.

"I walked away to say hi to a few people and I come back and you're in my seat." Bridgette joked.

"My bad, B. Here," I said, motioning for her to take the seat as I stood up. There was a single empty chair two tables away. I went and grabbed it and brought it back to our group.

"What you drinking on?" She asked.

"Just some cognac."

"Shit. That's that brown liccka. That can only mean one thing. Wanna talk?"

At first, I shook my head no. But on second thought. She was one of Evette's closest friends. If anyone could tell me something, it would be her. "Hold that thought. What you drinking? I asked.

"Just a cocktail."

I waved at the hostess. She came right over to take our orders. I gave her my card and told her to run a tab for the table.

"Now, where were we?"

"Shit, you tell me. You, the one deep in thought, sitting in the corner nursing Remy."

I took a deep breath, and choosing my words carefully, I asked Bridgette what was up with her girl.

I listened to Bridgette talk. She didn't say anything I didn't already know. I was expecting her to give a full confessional. Just hearing her say what I knew to be true eased my mind and my heart. I think that was what scared me the most. It was the fact of her calling me another nigga's name. Was it fucked up, yeah. But hell, I had been called worse. It was what it implied. I couldn't even allow myself to think about it let alone say it. My heart couldn't take that kind of rejection. None of which I disclosed to Bridgette.

Either Bridgette was a good liar, or everything she said matched up with what I knew. Being this close to Bridgette, I guess I never paid attention to how attractive she was. Her eyes were a deep gray color. They were hypnotizing. She pulled me in with every word she spoke. Bridgette had always been cool with me. I knew she had reservations about me at first. But I'd like to think I won her over. Besides, at this moment, she was a good friend. Not just to Evette, but to me.

We sat there drinking and laughing. She was quite funny. Bridgette was the company I needed tonight. Without her, I would just be the guy in the corner looking helpless, still pondering texting my girl when I'm supposed to be out with the fellas. "Hey, you dance?"

"I know you not tryna get served out on the dance floor?"

"Just don't do me like your family doing, my boys. They out there looking tired." We laughed as we headed out there to join them.

The band had stated they had three more songs before their set ended. It was no harm in thanking Bridgette for being a good sport. Besides, I enjoyed dancing. Evette and I danced often when we went out. I loved holding her close to me in such a sensual way. We hadn't danced together since we returned from vacation. Not even around the house. The tension was too thick to get through. But this, it was a stress relief. Mike, Greg, and the ladies welcomed us to the dance floor. I turned around and danced with each of the ladies. By the end of the second song, I had made my way back over to Bridgette. The band slowed things down as they closed out their set.

I held my hand out for Brigette to take it. She did. It was innocent. I held her in a friendly embrace as we slow danced. Her slim, thick five - seven frame allowed me to wrap my arms around her effortlessly. I guess I never noticed just how cool she was. "Why are you single? " I asked.

"I haven't found the right guy for me. You know anyone?"

I looked over at Greg and Mike. And we both snickered.

"Don't worry about Evette. She will come around soon. Plus, the wedding is approaching fast. I'll be there to push her ass down the aisle if I have to. Just be patient." She whispered in my ear.

I smiled and kissed her on her forehead. "Thank you, B."

"No worries. I know she loves you. Plus, you're ok for a felon."

Oh, you got jokes"

"No. I just know a good guy when I see one. Deshawn, you're a good guy," she said as the song ended. Her perfume and her words sung to my heart.

"So I have your stamp of approval B?"

"Yeah, I guess." She laughed as she pulled away from my embrace. I watched as she and her family collected their things. Greg and Mike were busy chatting it up with them. I hope they got their digits. Mike and Greg better had closed the deal or I would not let them live this down. Come Monday, I hope I won't have to beg Brigette for her cousin's information. I paid our tab and put my card back in my wallet. It was the first time in hours that I looked at my phone. Luckily, there weren't any missed text messages from Evette. I would just hit her up later, or better yet, maybe I would just head that way. We all walked out of the lounge and into the cool air. I watched as the ladies made their way to their car. I gave Mike and Greg some dap before making my way over to my truck. The parking lot was nearly empty as I pulled out. I started to turn left but made a sharp right and headed home.

CHAPTER TWENTY-EIGHT

I had no business being here; I thought to myself. This wasn't my intention. Radir and I were in bed together in silence. There was just something about this man that had a terrible hold on me. After a few minutes, I was ready to leave. This couldn't happen anymore. Radir must have sensed my frustrations.

"Shit, I thought I fucked you good. If I didn't let me try again." He joked, pulling me back toward the bed.

"Stop Radir!" I yelled out.

"Yo Evette. What's up?

I paused. Before I knew what I was saying, I uttered." We can't do this anymore."

"Sure we can. You want me and I want you."

"No! I can't. I'm marrying Deshawn. He's the man who loves me. He's the one I need to be with."

"Do you love him?"

I didn't say anything.

"Or do you love me?"

I looked up at Radir, feeling sick that he would even ask me that.

"I used to love you. There was a time I would have done anything for you. But you through all that away."

"But I'm here now. I know I fucked up. But Baby. I'm here now. Tell me you love me. A love like ours doesn't just end. I know you feel it. I feel it. Every time I see you. Just thinking about you. When I hold you in my arms. When I'm inside of you. Tell me you feel it too?"

"I can't do this anymore, Radir. I have to do what's right for me. Deshawn is a good guy. He loves me,"

"But do you love him? I know he can't do the things I can do for you. For fuck's sake, he's a garbage man! There is no future for you in that. Shit, you told me he's a felon. You can't be serious? You can't love him. Baby, tell me you love me the way I love you. This, what you and I have, is real. It's sustainable. You can build something on this. We have history. You can't just throw that away for the trashman."

"You left me. You choose her over me. You threw away what we had. And just when my life is right again, here you come. I can't love you. My heart won't let me. I'm marrying Deshawn. We can't do this anymore." I said, as I continued to get dressed.

"You can't be serious. I been fucking you down for the past six months. Not once did you scream out his name? Baby, only I can make you feel that good. Plus, baby, we make sense. Were educated, we have matching bank accounts. What can he do for you that I can't?"

There was silence. I knew on paper Radir and I made the better couple. But Deshawn loved me. I knew he did. What have I done? The tears streamed down my face. All this time, what I needed was right in front of me. What a fool I had been. I thought to myself as I gathered the rest of my belongings up and headed for the door.

"Evette, don't do this. You're making a mistake."

"Radir, why did you come back?"

"Huh?"

"Why did you come back after all this time? It's been eight years six since you broke my heart. Why did you come back?"

Radir looked stunned that I had asked him this question. He ran his hands over his face as he stood there in his boxer briefs.

"Well?!" I cried out.

His sigh, said it all. I turned to go walk out the door when he pulled my arm.

"Sharmaine told me you had moved on. She told me that you were still in love with me. I had been broken things off with what's her name. Sharmaine said you would welcome me back. I wasn't sure at first. That night in Chicago, you acted as if you never wanted to speak to me again. But seeing you brought back all those memories. I never stopped loving you. You looked hella good that night. You lost some weight; your confidence was so sexy. I remembered what it was like being with you. Plus, Sharmaine told me to keep trying. So, I pursued you full force."

"So that night in Chicago at the club. Sharmaine told you I would be there?"

"Yeah, she told me you were in town shopping. That I should surprise you."

"Wait, so you and her planned this?"

"Sort of. But It doesn't matter. We reconnected. Nothing's changed. There is still a lot of love between us. You know it, and so do I."

I felt sick listening to the words he spoke. Why would Sharmaine do this to me? She was supposed to be my girl. She knew how much Radir hurt me. Why would she play me like this? I felt nauseous. And without warning, I vomited all over the hardwood floor.

After things calmed down and Radir and I cleaned up the mess I made. Without saying a word, I exited his condo. I took the elevator down to the parking ramp. Preparing to make the forty-five-minute drive down US 131 Highway with Radir's words ringing loud in my ear. Sharmaine, Him. How could I be so gullible? Did he even love? Why should I care? It was over. As I approached my car, I noticed a familiar face leaning against the driver's side door. What the fuck?

"Umm. Excuse me, Cam, right? Why are you leaning against my car at this hour of the night?" I said with my hand on my bear spray. I had pulled it out my purse when I was in the elevator. A girl could never be too careful at this hour. First, I had no business being all the way in Grand Rapids, but the last thing I needed was for someone to try some shit with me. This must be my lucky night. First Radir, now this nigga, who I had no clue what the fuck he wanted, nor did I care.

"Hey Evette. Funny catching you here this time of the night. You're not staying the night?"

"Excuse me." I looked at him, annoyed he would dare ask me some shit like that. "I'm not sure why you're out here, nor do I care. Get the fuck off my car before I spray your ass." I said as I held up the small but deadly can with my finger ready to press down.

"I mean no harm." He said with both hands in the air as if to show me he was clean. "I just thought to myself, what would Deshawn do if he knew about you and Radir?"

"How the fuck do you know about Deshawn?" The level of regret sunk deep down and covered me again as the nausea set in again. I could feel my heart in my throat as Cam asked if I was ok.

"Yes, I'm good." I lied. "How do you know Deshawn?"

"De and I go way back. We like family. He didn't tell you about me. Why am I not surprised."

"What do you want?"

"Nothing yet. But I know fucking two guys when you're supposed to be in a committed relationship is a dangerous situation to be in. You need to be careful. If Deshawn finds out.. well let's just say when he finds out it won't be good for anyone."

"Deshawn won't find out because there isn't anything to find out about."

"If you say so. But I recall, Radir said you were his girl. You leaving this condo at this ungodly hour smells like a booty call to me. But what do I know?"

I could feel the second round of vomit inching its way up my throat. My mouth salivated with the salty sensation, and as Cam looked me over, I turned and threw up once more. Shit. This just wasn't my night.

"Oh shit. Evette, you're pregnant?" He laughed. "This is just great. Imma let you handle yourself. I'll be in touch. Imma be an uncle. Hey maybe, you can give me some of that pregnancy pussy you like to share so badly. If it's good enough for De and Radir, hell, it's good enough for me," he joked as he walked away into the night.

I turned to make sure he was gone. I couldn't stop vomiting long enough to spray him. How the hell did he know I would be here? Was he watching me? Was Deshawn watching me? Is that who sent him? Could I be pregnant? Holy shit. I had so many questions and a long ass ride home to rethink my actions. What the fuck was I going to do?

CHAPTER TWENTY-NINE

With roses and calla lilies in hand, I head over to Evette's. There was still time for me to salvage this weekend. Bridgette's words echoed in my ear; be patient with Evette. I knew she had been in a hurtful relationship prior to me. I never knew who the dude was, but the damage he left behind had a lasting impression on her heart. When we first started dating, I gave Evette every opportunity to see that I was a man of my word. My actions matched everything I said. Slowly, I gained her trust. Not once did she want for anything with me. Yeah, I still hadn't told her about my fortune. I guess I wanted to make sure that our relationship lasted. I knew the money issue was a big deal to Evette. Finances had come up a few times, but she never really wanted to know much more than I could afford whatever it was she was asking for. I woke up this morning thinking now was the time to let her know that I really did match her swag. Lay out all my cards on the table. Maybe this would ease the stress of getting married.

I arrived at her parking garage in my vehicle. Her favorite Starbucks drink, the flowers, and the takeout breakfast from

Nina's were in my hands. I waved to the guys at the front lobby desk and headed upstairs. I had my keys on me but rang the bell so I wouldn't alarm her. After the second ring and no answer on the security door device. I took my keys out and let myself in. Placing the items on the kitchen counter, I called out to her, "E baby, where you at?" I heard a faint cry coming from her bedroom. I walked back to where the muffled sounds were coming from. I found Evette nestled around the bathroom toilet. She looked like she had been through it. "Evette, what's wrong, baby?" I asked.

"I don't feel well," she spoke in a weakened state.

"Oh, baby. I gotchu." I said as I picked her up and carried her back to bed. I disrobed her and made her comfortable in bed. Pulling the trash can closer to the bed, I got a glass of water for her and climbed into bed next to her. I held her tight in my arms until she fell asleep.

Once Evette was sleeping, I cleaned and disinfected the bathroom. I found some decorative vases in the kitchen cabinet. Arranged the flowers and placed them in the room for her to see when she woke up. I picked up the rest of the house and lit a new candle from Bath and Body Works. Turning the television on in the front room, I heated my breakfast up and chilled as I watched ESPN. Just as I was finishing up my takeout. I could hear the constant humming of what sounded like a cell phone. Searching through the cushions of the couch, I found Evette's cell phone. One alert stated she was at one percent of her battery life. The other alert I noticed caught my eye.

> **Radir-**
> Can we talk about last night?

    The phone went dead. I sat it on the charger in the kitchen as I picked up my keys and left without checking in on her.

CHAPTER THIRTY

I made my way to the Bronson Methodist hospital. My gynecologist was on the second floor of the hospital. After leaving Radir's condo, I had been throwing up nonstop. I prayed Cam was wrong. But with all the stress I had been under, I couldn't recall the last time I had my period. I checked in at the receptionist's desk. Taking a seat in the waiting area, I thumbed through the maternity magazines that laced the table. The thought of being someone's mother scared the living shit out of me. Not to mention I wasn't sure if it would be Deshawn's or Radir's at this point if I were pregnant. I blocked Radir, but that didn't stop him from reaching out or coming by my office. I told Tamika that under no circumstances was he allowed in the building so security always stopped his attempts to enter. Deshawn was acting funny. And being that I wasn't feeling well, the last thing I had time for was running behind him. All the more reason to get this test over with and be able to move on.

"Evette, Dr. Candon will see you now," the nurse stated as the doors opened, and she escorted me down the hallway and into room C. "Take everything except your underwear off. Put this robe on when you're done. I'll be back to take your vitals in a few minutes" she instructed. I did as I was instructed. I sat on the exam table and waited for her to return. My empty stomach growled, but I dared not eat anything and risk throwing up in the car on my way here. The nurse returned and took my vitals.

"Everything looks wonderful. Blood pressure was slightly high, but I'll check it again in a few. Dr. Candon will be in shortly. If it's possible, can we get a urine sample while you wait?" She pointed to the specimen cup with the orange top. "The bathroom is down the hall on your left."

I grabbed the cup and headed to the restroom. Following the instructions on the bathroom wall, I wrapped the cup in paper towels, washed my hands, and departed. I returned to my room and Dr. Candon was waiting for me.

"Evette. How are you?"

I hated that question. Like I wouldn't be here if everything was fine. I didn't say that out loud. I knew it was just my nerves getting the best of me. "I wish I could say I was ok. I've been throwing up, I'm tired, and I can't keep anything down. Plus, I can't recall the last time I had a period." I confessed.

"What has been going on in your life that you can't recall your last menstrual cycle?"

"Stress from work, and my personal life is a hot mess."

"Well, let's take a look at a few things. Lay back on the table for me. Feet in the stirrups. I'm going to conduct your annual pap smear and run some test."

I did as I was told. Dr. Candon was quiet as she worked. I could feel the poking and pressure from her conducting the exam. She gathered a few samples. And when she was done, removed her instruments and told me I could scoot back up on the table. She then placed her icy hands on my stomach. She pressed down a few times before asking me to sit up. With her stethoscope placed on my back and chest, I breathed in and out at her command. By this time, the nurse had returned with a few print outs. Dr. Candon looked them over and smiled.

"Evette, you are good and pregnant. You are about fourteen weeks along. I can't confirm this until I see the ultrasound. But you are for sure pregnant."

I heard her, but I could not believe it. How could I be so careless? And to be this far along. How did I not notice the changes in my body? Whose baby was I carrying? I had unprotected sex with both Deshawn and Radir. I assumed that my birth control would have been enough. Hell, now that I think about it, I'm not sure I was even taking them regularly. There was just so much going on. I was too old and educated to be having a moment like this. I knew better.

"Evette did you hear?" Dr. Candon asked.

"I'm sorry. I zoned out for a moment. All of this has taken me by surprise."

"I bet. The last time we spoke, you didn't want kids. Your career was your baby. And with you being so far long, terminating the pregnancy is risky. We only have a brief window of opportunity to conduct the procedure. I want to get a sonogram done today so we can confirm dates and talk through next steps."

I just shook my head yes. I was at a loss for words.

I left the hospital with all kinds of informational pamphlets. The rest of the day, I was in a complete haze. Returning to work was out of the question. I wanted to call Deshawn, but what would I say? Bridgette was at work. I wasn't speaking with

Sharmaine. That only left one person for me to speak with. And against my better judgement, I headed towards Grand Rapids, hoping that Radir was available.

While I was in my car making the drive-up US 131, my cell phone rang. It was connected to the Bluetooth feature in my car. I didn't recognize the number and hesitated to answer. Thinking it could be work related or even the doctor's office, I took the chance and answered.

"Hello"

"Evette. So what's the good word?" the wicked voice spoke through the car speakers.

I knew the voice. It was Cam. His words for our previous encounter haunted me even days later. "How did you get my number?"

"Shid! That's the least of your concerns. Do you know who the daddy of that baby is yet? I mean, unless there is a third nigga in the mix, I've narrowed it down to Deshawn and Radir." He laughed.

"What do you want with me?"

"Now that's the first smart thing you've said since we met. I want Deshawn back. I need that nigga to do a job for me. And you're gonna help me."

"I will do no such thing. I can't make Deshawn do anything he doesn't want to do."

"That's where you're wrong. You will. Hell, you betta get that nigga to do it or else your little secret becomes public knowledge. And knowing my brother... let's just say two strikes and this time he might not get out of that cell anytime soon."

"I can't.."

"Bitch you will. No I'm not asking. And believe me, getting access to you is easier than you think. I wouldn't want anything to happen to that pretty face of yours or that baby. Besides, you still haven't given me any of that sweet pussy yet."

His words scared me to silence. Usually, I had a smart comeback or a sarcastic remark. Cam frightened me. Men like him have crossed my path before. His words had power, and he followed through on his threats without hesitation. I refrained from crying, knowing it would only excite Cam further. I had fucked up big time. There was no way out of this, and I absolutely didn't want Radir to be discovered by Deshawn. I did the only thing I could; I agreed to help him.

"That's what I thought. Here... Meet me at this address. See you in thirty."

Cam hung the phone up before I could reply. I guess I was heading to Grand Rapids to see him and not Radir.

I couldn't believe that I found myself in this predicament. How could I have been so stupid? I wanted to scream, but what good would that do for me? I was already knee deep in my shit. The only saving grace would be if this baby was Deshawn's. The baby had to be his. What am I even thinking about this for? I'm not even sure if I'm going to keep it. Right now, I need to focus. I was waiting for Cam. He instructed me to text him once I pulled into the driveway. I was somewhere on the east side of the city. It was peaceful in the neighborhood. The house I pulled up to was an older home with neatly manicured landscaping. As soon as I texted Cam, a young lady opened the front door to the house and stood on the porch waving me in.

Reluctantly, I exited the car, locked it, and followed the girl into the house. She flopped down on the beige couch, leaving me to close the door behind me.

"I'm here to see Cam," I stated.

The young lady just looked me over as she lit the end of her meticulously rolled blunt. She took two poofs and blew her smoke in my direction as I stood there in the doorway. Finally, I could hear Cam's voice coming from the other end of the house. Emerging from behind closed doors, he greeted me with a sly grin. His presence suggested that I was way in over my head dealing with him. I wish I had the courage to come clean and let Deshawn know what I had done. But I risked losing him and now that I may be pregnant with his child, I couldn't take the chance that he wouldn't love me.

"Humm." He sighed, walking up the stairs. He turned around and looked at me. "Well? What are you waiting for? Come on."

I flowed behind him as he led me down the hallway and into the room at the end of the house.

"Take a seat."

"I'll stand"

He shrugged his shoulders as if he didn't care. I stood there, body tense as I watched Cam pull an envelope out of the desk that sat in the middle of the room.

"You book smart. Read this and figure out a way to get Deshawn to get me the information I need."

I opened the envelope and read over the document. I stopped midway down the first page. Shaking my head, confused. "What is this?" I asked.

Cam smirked as he leaned against the desk. "Ya boy took something from me and I want it back. I need him to deliver that to the people we owe."

"Who is we? DeShawn has nothing to do with this."

"Deshawn took something from me. I didn't realize what he had done until he got locked up. I want it back. So, we have a problem. Until I get it back, it ain't just my ass on the line. "

"Why can't you just ask him for it? Why am I here? I have nothing to do with this."

"Don't you think I've tried reaching out to him? Nah, he on some other shit. His emotional ass too busy running after you. Look. All I want is my shit back. I don't care how you do it, just get him to make that delivery."

Cam stood there in his throwback sweatsuit. His jacket was open, exposing me to his bare chest. I could hear in his voice that he meant business. The way his chest and breathing pattern tightened as he spoke cause my muscles to tense up even more. I folded up the envelope and placed it in my purse. He watched me as I stood there waiting for him to dismiss me. But he didn't. We stood in the silent room as my nerves caused me to quake with fear.

"Chill Evette. I'm not going to hurt you. Yet anyway, "he half joked.

"Why involve me?"

"I already told you. Plus, you made it easy for me."

"Easy? How?"

"C'mon ma, you fucking two dudes I do business with. Shit was bound to catch up with you. You don't seem like the type that can pull finessing two niggas off like that. You're more of a one-man kinda girl."

"You know nothing about me."

"You think the first time I met you was that night in the restaurant? Nah ma. I peeped you out the minute I found out that Deshawn was out and you were dating. I make it my bidness to know things. It just so happens that you kept popping up. First Deshawn, then Radir. Like I said, easy."

I huffed at his insinuation. He didn't know me. Hell, these days I barely knew myself. I thought internally.

"Let me ask you something. How well do you know Deshawn? I mean, really know him?"

I just stared at him. I just really wanted him to let me go. But he continued to speak.

"That's what I thought. That nigga don't know you and you certainly don't know him. I know one thing; I see what him and ole boy see in you. Yeah, I see you. I know your type." He said, as his eyes roamed over my body.

"Full hips, lips and breast. And you got brains. You got both dem niggas hit. I bet you give hella good head. I'm not going to lie, I'm jealous. And Yo, if that shit don't work with either of them, you know with the baby and all, I'll be here, waiting to see what you taste like. But seriously, ma, let me, stop fucking with you. Handle that. I'll be in touch."

I was frozen. The thought of him touching me scared me senseless. I watched as he walked up to me and passed me by. My breathing heaved at his words. Cam had a presence about him I just could not imagine Deshawn embodying. Sure, Deshawn was raw around the edges at times. But nothing like Cam. I heard the door open. I turned to look at Cam who was standing with his gun in his hand. The serious look on his face told me the meeting was over. He meant every word he spoke to me and the flashing of his gun echoed his sentiments. I trudged past him. Hurrying down the hallway and out the front door. I didn't even have time to see if the young lady who escorted me in was still lounging on the couch. I just ran out the door, got in my car and drove away.

CHAPTER THIRTY-ONE

Evette was quiet after dinner today. She barely touched her food. I just assumed it was because she still hadn't been feeling well. I was going between my place and hers. When I spent the night with her, she refused to allow me to be intimate with her. This added more suspension to what was going on with her. She would try to blame it on not feeling well. Which led to us arguing. The chemistry between us was off. It seemed like everything I did upset her. And everything she displayed to me added to my frustration. If I didn't stay at her place, she was pissed. If I stayed the night, she wanted me gone. I just couldn't get it right. My patience was wearing thin and my overactive imagination was taking over.

Our wedding was just two months away. I still haven't told Evette about the money. We were operating separately. Nothing was coming together. I almost wanted to postpone the wedding, but every time I mentioned it to Evette, she wasn't having it. She appeared to be putting on a few pounds. I thought it was sexy as hell, but she seemed annoyed that I noticed. Plus, there was still the lingering feeling I had in my gut that told me something wasn't right with Evette.

The only saving grace of the evening was that Bridgette stopped by. She and Evette had to go over a few details for the wedding. I just left them two to do whatever they needed to do. The only time I was bothered or asked a question was when they needed access to my credit card or to confirm minor details about the groomsmen. I made myself comfortable on the couch and tuned out their conversation. Before long, I had dozed off.

"Man, you ready to take that plunge?" Mike asked as we finished eating our lunch.

"That's right, the wedding is right around the corner," Greg said.

I was in the zone and had tuned everything around me out. I didn't hear Mike and Greg's banter until Greg nudged me out of my thoughts.

"You good?" he asked.

"Yeah man, just shit with the wedding."

"Don't go getting cold feet now."

"Yeah, the last thing we need is for your ass to back out now."

"Naw. Never that," I lied. Maybe for the first time in my relationship, I questioned if this was something I should be doing. No matter what I did to fix whatever the fuck was wrong in my relationship with Evette, nothing seemed to work. I was envisioning years of marriage existing in this space. The misery of living like that had me feeling some kind of way. But I had to save face. At least for right now. "Nothing could keep me from walking down that aisle and marrying my babe." I lied again.

"If you say so" Mike laughed.

"Yup. That's what I know."

We finished up our route and ended the day as quickly as it had started. By the time we pulled into the sanitation depot, it was well past six. I said my peace to the fellas and clocked out. I was headed back to my place to wash up and get changed when my cell phone rang. As much as I wanted to send the caller to voicemail, I opted to answer it instead.

"Hey baby" Evette called out.

"Hey sexy lady." She sounded like she was in a good mood.

"Are you headed this way?"

"I was about to stop by my place and wash up. Why?"

"Can you come here first? I have something for you."

"Sure. I'll be there in fifteen."

"Good. I'll see you soon."

The call ended.

What could she possibly have for me? My current mind state wouldn't allow me to conceive that it was something positive. Knowing her, it had something to do with the wedding. A wedding I wasn't sure should even be happening. Like a good fiancé, I made a U-turn at the next cross street and turned my car around. I headed toward Evette's hoping tonight would differ from the past few months.

We I arrived at Evette's condo; she greeted me with a warm kiss. This action had become foreign to me. It was something that she used to do on a regular but had been absent from our routine. "Hey baby" I greeted her matching her excitement.

"Here, come with me."

I followed Evette to the bedroom. The room was laced with candles and flower petals. The masculine aroma coming from the three wicked candle filled the air. Evette guided me to the tub. I could see the steam from the water etched on the mirror. She seductively ran her fingers over my bare body. Her touch sent shockwaves through my soul. I had missed this form of intimacy from her. Although shocked by her gesture, I dare not ask what brought this on for fear that it would kill the mood. I just stayed in the moment.

Evette toured the contours of my body with the hot water drenched wash cloth. I closed my eyes and relaxed, knowing I was in excellent hands. Without my knowing, Evette had undressed and joined me in the tub. She squatted down on my lap. Her back pressed into my chest. In silence, we just enjoyed the warmth of the water and the syncing of our heartbeats. This is what I missed most over the last few months. Evette seemed so vulnerable and at peace. I wanted her to trust that I would do nothing to jeopardize her faith in me.

"I have something to tell you."

"You know you can tell me anything. What is it?"

"I'm... I'm pregnant"

I opened my eyes to see Evette's eyes searching mine for an expression. Slowly, a smile crept across my face. I saw her facial muscles soften as my reaction became more obvious.

"Are you sure?"

"Yes. I'm very pregnant."

"We're going to have a baby. I'm going to be a dad?" I asked, placing my hand on her firm belly.

Evette turned around and faced me. The flickering candles highlighted her silhouette. How did I not notice the changes in her? Her plump breast looked so enticing as her nipples stood at attention like fruit waiting to be harvested. Evette's hips were full and her belly protruded, forming a slight bump. Her beauty was unmatched. My eyes searched over her for a reason to find fault with her, but hearing her announcement and seeing her in this state made me forget all about the past few months. All I wanted was to love her. Show her I could be the man of her dreams.

I held Evette in my arms all night long. The excitement of the evening made me ever want to let her go. I stayed up all night imagining life with her and our unborn child. I never imagined that I would find love and be someone's father. That dream died with Vivian. I promised myself that living in a fantasy world would only lead to heartache and pain, especially with me doing time in prison. Vivian held so much of my heart that I refused to allow anyone or thing to occupy that space that way again. That was until Evette came along. And now this. I think I smiled all night long. It didn't even bother me that the alarm clock went off and I was wide awake. It was the first time since Evette declared her pregnancy that I released her from my grasp.

I dressed and got ready for work. I made a healthy breakfast for Evette and myself. I kissed Evette goodbye before heading out the door. Leaving her is something I hate to do, but I knew the sooner I started my day, the quicker my return would be. Besides, nothing would keep me away from the woman carrying my seed. For the first time, I felt like everything was right with the world.

The fellas and I finished our route early today. They clowned me for wanting to work through lunch, but they agreed. I had only one thing on my mind, and that was getting back to Evette.

The thought of her last night and the baby she was carrying warmed my heart. We pulled into the sanitation depot; I clocked out and immediately headed to Evette's. I was halfway there when I received a message on my cell phone.

> We need to meet up. Are you free?

I started to ignore the message, but knew I needed to take care of this. I turned the car around and headed in the opposite direction.

"Siri text back: I'm headed to you now. Be there in twenty minutes."

Siri–Text completed.

CHAPTER THIRTY-TWO

I feel like someone had lifted a weight off of me. Finally, telling Deshawn about the baby and seeing his reaction made everything feel so right. I decided I would not tell Radir about the baby. It would only complicate matters. Besides, in my mind, the baby was Deshawn's. It had to be. So, I told him. It felt so right. He held me in his arms all night long. I forgot how special he made me feel. The way he loved on me. The way he kissed my belly bump made me realize he was all I ever needed. I had played myself, thinking that Radir and I would ever have anything other than history. A tainted one at that. I had decided. My future was with Deshawn. I needed to officially end things with Radir.

After work, I made my way up to Grand Rapids. I parked in the visitor parking space to Radir's condo. Radir had given me a spare key and the access codes to enter the complex. He wasn't expecting me, which was fine. I wanted to return his keys and end things face to face. I knew if he knew I was coming, he would try to make this into something it wasn't. His car was parked in his designated space. Walking past it and taking the elevator up to the sixth floor, I rehearsed everything I needed to say. I was going to keep it simple and to the point. I approached his condo and knocked. There was no answer. I started to leave, but let myself in, thinking he might be in a meeting or sleeping.

Searching the condo, at first, I could not find Radir. I went to his office first, thinking he might be working. I made my way upstairs. As I approached the door, I thought I heard Radir talking on the phone. I opened the door a little wider. I gasped at the sight of him and Sharmaine fucking. It took me a few seconds to register what I was seeing. My presence caused them to stop. I sprinted down the stairs. Radir called out after me. I didn't stop. Tears formed in my eyes. How could she? He? I couldn't believe I had been such a fool, I thought to myself as I angrily pushed for the elevator doors to close before Radir could make it to me.

I made it to my car, just as I did, I could see Radir running behind my car as I pulled off. The image of him and Sharmaine played over and over in my mind the entire ride home. I wanted to forget that I even allowed myself to be sucked into his world again. I should have known better. He hadn't changed one bit. I expected this behavior from him. It was like déjà vu all over again. But Sharmaine. She was supposed to be my friend. I had told her everything about me and Radir. Hell, she was there from the very beginning. Sharmaine knew how much I loved him. "How could she?" I cried to myself.

The entire ride home, Radir was blowing up my phone. I declined all thirty of his attempts. Sharmaine even tried calling me. I was done with her and completely through with Radir.

There was nothing left to say. All I wanted was to get home. I wanted to forget that I even fucked with Radir. I wanted Deshawn to erase all memories of him from my heart and mind. The last phone call that came across the car dashboard I really wanted to ignore, but I couldn't. I answered it.

"Did you handle that?"

"I need more time"

"You running out of time and my patience is running thin with you,"

"I said I would do it. And I will,"

"You betta."

The phone went dead.

Fuck!!!

CHAPTER THIRTY-THREE

Evette and I were enjoying a nice dinner at a bistro downtown, not too far from her condo. Ever since Evette told me about the pregnancy, she had been a different person. She was more attentive, and mild tempered. She was still her feisty self, but I could tell she was fully invested in our relationship. Which was completely the opposite of the last few months. I'd like to think that work had become manageable for her and the stress she was under had subsided. Evette was home every day by five in the evening. We ate dinner together. Talked about our future bundle of joy and the impeding wedding plans. So, tonight is special. I wanted to give Evette the one thing I knew she needed to see: that I was serious about our future.

After dessert, I handed Evette an envelope. She was hesitant to open it. But I encouraged her to with an excited look on my face. It was time she knew I could take care of her the way she needed me to. I watched as she read over my financial statements. She would occasionally look up at me and then back to one of the fourteen pages.

"Wait, what?" she questioned.

"It's all there."

"How is this possible?"

Pausing before speaking. I had told Evette about my past. I was as transparent as I could be. Not disclosing all the details of my sketchy past, I admitted, "I stashed away money for a rainy day. The streets don't have a retirement plan for old dudes like me. So, I invested what I could. Unlike my counterparts, I didn't need to be the flashiest nigga on the corner. My rep was all I needed. What you're reading is what I've been sitting on."

"But it states that you're a millionaire. How could this be? You're a garbage man. That's what you told me."

"That's my job. It's not who I am. I had to prove to myself that I could make a decent, honest living. I had already given too much of my life to the streets. Once I left prison, I promised myself that I would do whatever it took not to go back. I was lucky to get that job. Do you know how difficult it is for someone like me with a felony charge strapped to their back? That's why I don't care what people think about what I do. I know a lot of good dudes that work for the sanitation department. They make a good living. Ain't no shame in that."

"Wait, is that how you could afford my wedding dress, the trip to Antigua, oh the black card? You have a black card. I remember seeing it that time in the boutique. All this time. You could have told me."

"I'm telling you now. You don't have to worry, I gotchu. You and our baby won't have anything to worry about."

Evette started crying uncontrollably. I kneeled down beside her. "It's ok E. Please forgive me for taking so long to share this with you. I just wanted to make sure you knew you didn't have to worry about a damn thing with me. I thought comforting her would reassure her of my intentions. But she just cried into my shoulder. "I love you Evette," I whispered. She just held on to me. I was hoping her tears were that of joy. My financial stability was always a concern for her, although I never gave her a reason to doubt me. She had proof that I was that guy. And now she knew how. I waved for the waiter to bring me the check. He obliged. I paid for our night out and took Evette home.

Over the next few weeks, Evette seemed relieved. I wasn't sure if it was the financial burden being lifted or the baby. But she radiated with joy. We started house shopping now that we had completed the final plans for the wedding. Evette wanted to be in the new home before the baby was born. I gave her free range of figuring out what she wanted. When she asked how much could she spend, I told her whatever it took to make her happy. She deserved to have the home of her dreams. Things were finally falling into place for me. My heart was full of everything I thought I had lost. The truth was, I had never known love like this. Evette gave me everything I was missed being locked up all those years. My freedom had meaning.

CHAPTER THIRTY-FOUR

It was finally the evening of our wedding shower. Bridgette threw a co-ed wedding shower for Evette and me. I didn't think it was a good idea. She had just had a bridal shower a few weeks ago. There was no need to do anything for me. But she insisted. To my surprise, the fellas were down with the idea and had planned on attending the party. I played along and did what the ladies asked me to do. Evette had coordinated outfits for us to wear. She looked stunning in her fitted sequined dress. It camouflaged her baby bump, but I knew it was there. I wasn't sure who all knew about the pregnancy. Evette said that she would tell a few family members and her closest friends, but we agreed to wait until after the wedding to make the formal announcement.

Together, in our formal attire, Evette and I arrived at the venue that was hosting the event. I must admit, Bridgette out did herself. The space was decorated tastefully. Bridgette spared no expense, and I was sure my credit card would tell me just how much this party cost. But it didn't matter as long as Evette smiled.

I would do anything to make sure this lady was happy. The guests had already started arriving. Evette and I mingled with our friends and family. I spotted my boys over at the bar and eventually made my way over to them.

"De man, this is nice."

"Right, and he even cleaned up good," Mike and Greg clowned as I approached them. We greeted each other in our usual way. I continued making my way across the room and greeting our guests. My sister and her husband were present, which made me even more ecstatic that they supported me and Evette. I went over to their table and sat with them for a few minutes, promising to bring Evette over for dinner soon. I noticed the room filled up quickly. Everyone that loved and supported me and Evette was in attendance. It was great seeing so many familiar faces. Vivian and her husband even made it tonight to celebrate our union. I greeted Vivian and Timothy and thanked them for coming. She smiled. I knew she was genuinely happy for me, but under different circumstances the what if lingered in her eyes.

The DJ was playing all the right tunes to keep the atmosphere going. We were getting ready to gather for dinner when I noticed uninvited guests enter the room. Cam and another gentleman started to mingle with other guests. I tried to keep my cool. This wasn't the place or time for this nigga to get under my skin. My sister and Vivian noticed Cam's presence as well. They both looked at me and headed in my direction as I headed over in his direction.

"What are you doing here?" I snapped.

"Hey Bruh, I just came to extend my congratulations to you and the soon to be Mrs."

"This is a private event. I'mma need you to walk your ass back out the same way you came in."

"That's no way to talk to family. I just wanted to give you my blessings. Oh, yeah, where's my manners? Radir, this is my brother, Deshawn. Deshawn, Radir."

There was an awkward pause and a sinister grin on Cam's face. I sized up Radir as he stood there resisting my glares. He was dressed in a well-tailored black suit. His five eleven frame stood parallel to mine. I felt a heat rising within me. What were the coincidences that I would hear that name again? I watched the look on Cam's face as he entertained what could be going through my mind. Cam knew me all too well. He also knew I wouldn't make a scene. Not here, not now. The anger that arose within me had me on edge. I hadn't noticed that Vivian and my sister had made their way over to me.

"Hey Viv. You looking good. Deniece, long time no see girl," Cam said, acknowledging the women behind me. Bridget invited the men to take a seat. Before I could interject, Cam immediately took the opportunity to slip away as he followed Bridgette. I watched as he and Radir took their places among the rest of the guests.

"You good?" Vivian asked.

"Yea." I said through clenched teeth.

"What is he doing here?" my sister questioned.

"I'm not sure. But I'll keep an eye on him." I stated as I walked away.

For the rest of the evening, my guard was up. I smiled through the formalities, but the only thing on my mind was what was Cam up to. You would think that ass whoppin I gave him was enough for him to back off. I knew that nigga was strapped. I wasn't. I studied him and Radir the whole evening. Evette seemed uncomfortable. My attention turned to her as I caught her making eye contact with Radir and Cam. I asked her if she knew them and she said no. But I could tell she wasn't telling the truth. She hesitated and refused to look me in the eye, something Evette never did when I spoke to her. I hoped to God that I was wrong, but my instincts told me she knew one or both men. Cam, I could understand. But who was this Radir character?

For the rest of the night, Cam behaved himself, which was out of character for him. It was the shy, sinister grin on his face that let me know he was certainly up to no good. I'm not sure what role Radir played in his antics, but I was watching both of them. Evette's jittery behavior continued into the evening. Her discomfort set off alarm bells inside my head. I observed Evette's movements as she interacted with family and friends to avoid Cam and Radir, making it seem like a well-coordinated dance. By now the Hennessy was whispering dangerous thoughts into my psyche. The dark thoughts and images had me frowning behind my wicked smile.

My boys must've sensed my change in demeanor. They asked me to follow them outside for a celebratory smoke as they waved a box of cigars at me. Reluctant to take my eyes off Evette, Cam and that nigga, they ushered me outside.

"Yo D, you good?"

'Yea man."

"You sure? Cause if looks could kill.."

Interrupting Mike's train of thought, I continued, "I said I was good." There was a long pause. Taking a deep breath, I turned to face the group of men that clearly had my back, even when I wasn't as forthcoming with information. "Fellas, pass that cigar and let's toast to this evening." I expected the bewildered look on their faces considering I was just about to tear into them for questioning me just minutes earlier. "Naw for real, Fellas, I'm so happy that you came out to celebrate with me. I appreciate and love all yall." I manned up and confessed. In their company, the stress of the situation seemed to calm down. Besides, today was supposed to be a joyous occasion.

After smoking a few cigars and cracking jokes with the crew at my expense, I headed back into the event hall. My eyes roamed over the faces of the guests as I searched the crowd for Evette. She was nowhere to be found. Worse, I couldn't find Cam or Radir. And before I could react, that funny feeling in my gut was back.

CHAPTER THIRTY-FIVE

"What the Fuck Radir!"

"Look, it was not my idea to come here. Cam asked me to hang with him tonight. I did not know we would end up here. But I'm glad we did. You stopped returning my calls. I needed to see you."

"We said all we need to say to each other."

"So, you just gonna give up on us?"

"Deshawn loves me."

"Do you love him?" Radir asked me. I had avoided answering this question before when he asked. It was none of his business, besides I loved Deshawn. Was I in love with him? I'm not sure. I mean, my mouth wanted to answer yes, but looking into Radir's piercing eyes, my lips couldn't form the words I needed to say to convince him or myself. The sudden appearance of Cam broke the silence up.

"Secret lovers, yeah, that's what we are," he jokingly sang. Our locked gaze now focused on Cam and his antics. His wicked grin and smug look scared me as he made his way between Radir and I.

"Why are you here?"

"Aww, that's no way to greet a guest. After all, a woman in your situation needs to be careful. All this stress can't be good for the baby."

"Baby? What Baby?" Radir questioned.

"Oh, shit! He didn't know. Damn, that's fucked up Evette." Cam laughed.

"Are you pregnant, Evette? Is it mine?" Radir quizzed as he walked closer to me.

"Stop! Both of you. I can't do this right here. Not right now. Not with Deshawn here. Radir, I'll call you later. But you really do need to leave now. Cam, I'll..."

"You'll what? Time is up, sweetheart. I warned you what would happen if I didn't get my shit back."

"Cam I know. I just need a few more days. You can expect me to deliver on my promise. I just need a few more days." I begged.

"There are two things I can't stand, a beggin' bitch and a simp ass nigga. You better be happy you're carrying my nephew. That's your only saving grace. You got two days."

"Now, will you both leave?" I panicked as I watched the doorway, knowing Deshawn could walk back in from outside at any minute. I had to get Radir and Cam out of here.

"We're leaving. But if I don't get what I want in two forty-eight hours, I won't send a warning. I'll just rain down hail on you." Cam stated as he showed me the gun that was lodged on his hip. Cam didn't strike me as someone that cared that the room was full of people. He wouldn't hesitate to pull out his gun if he had to and use it. I struggled to believe that he and Deshawn were close friends at one point. Radir and I made eye contact as he passed by me. He didn't say a word as he left the event. And now he knew about the pregnancy, something I wasn't planning on telling him. I had less than two days to figure out how to get myself out of this mess.

"Deshawn has been acting distant. I can't figure out what is going on with him." I confided to CeCe and Bridgette over lunch.

"Maybe he just has a lot on his mind with the upcoming wedding."

"Yeah, girl. The way that man loves you, I'm sure it's nothing to worry about."

The comments from the ladies eased my mind for the moment. But I knew Deshawn. Something was bothering him. I tried to remember the last few days and the night of the bridal party to see if I had done something wrong. My attempts were unsuccessful. I knew there was no way he knew about my conversations with Cam, because then he would know about Radir. Luckily for me, it hadn't come to that yet.

Girl, did you hear me? Earth to Evette?"

I zoned in to hearing Bridgette laughing at me. "What? I'm sorry, ladies. I was thinking of wedding stuff." I lied. Something I was becoming all too good at.

"I said, what's going on with you and Sharmaine?"

CeCe and Bridgette were waiting for my reply. The group felt Sharmaine's absence, and the silence at the table was thick with anticipation as CeCe and Bridgette waited for my reply. Not wanting to disclose the fact that I just ended things with Radir, something I told them I was doing months ago, or that

Sharmaine was the one who set all of this in motion. I opted to lie again, as the truth just wasn't in me. The disappointment of my predicament was too much to bear. The last thing I needed was the judgmental stares from CeCe and Bridgette. " Nothing. I just haven't had time to connect with her."

"Well, I invited her to lunch today. She said she already had plans."

"I thought for sure we would have seen her at the party. "

"You know Sharmaine. She will come around when she is ready." I nonchalantly gestured as I took a sip of my mimosa. We finished up the lunch conversation with a last toast to the upcoming nuptials, which now were less than a month away. CeCe, Bridgette and I walk out of the Bistro together. We hugged each other and went our separate ways. I watched the ladies pull off in the separate vehicles before I drove off.

I pulled up to Radir's condo. There was a piece of me that just wanted to have the conversation with him over the phone. But I knew Radir would keep pushing. He was relentless that way. I was on borrowed time. With Radir knowing about the baby, I was going to have to make a convincing argument that it was Deshawn's and not his. I also had to deal with Cam. But I would figure that out after I handled Radir. I rang the doorbell, knowing he was home. His car was in the designated parking spot in the condo garage. I'd noticed it on my way into the building. There was no answer. Remembering where he kept the spare key. I reached into the light fixture, took the key, and let myself in.

Once inside, I could hear familiar voices coming from the direction of the bedroom. Slowly, I walked down the sterile hallway. Coming to the bedroom door. My heart sank deep into my stomach. I pushed open the door. Sharmaine straddled Radir as he held on to her chocolate toned body. The way their bodies collided in unison was something I thought was reserved for only Radir and me. I was wrong. My gasping for air broke through their moans as they both stopped in shock that I was standing there. Before either of them could move, I ran out of the condo, holding my stomaching and tears back. How could Sharmaine be so wicked! I thought to myself as my failed attempted to stay calm became a flood of emotions and tears. How could he? Why would they? So many questions raced through my mind as I pulled out of the garage and headed home.

CHAPTER THIRTY-SIX

After the party, I couldn't stop thinking about the uninvited guest. Not so much Cam, as I expect his grimy ass to try some shit. But that Radir nigga. Nothing about him set well with me. Even Evette's jittery behavior told me something was up. Then I got to thinking. I remember him stopping by Evette's place one night while I was cooking dinner. I thought he was a coworker. Now I know he and Evette didn't work together. Then they had the nerve to play that shit off like they never met. Just thinking about this shit had my blood boiling.

A while back, when I first got that uneasy feeling, I hired a private investigator. He was only supposed to be doing some intel on Cam, but when Evette started acting strange, I asked him to look into her. It wasn't that I thought she would ever be unfaithful. The thought really never crossed my mind until now. I wanted to make sure Evette was someone I could share my fortune with. After all, I just disclosed to her I was worth millions. Evette never really asked about my money, but her sly comments about the work I did made me feel like she thought I couldn't afford to take care of her. But before the private investigator could tell me anything about his findings, I pulled the plug. I thought my insecurities were getting the best of me. The whole thing with Evette had me feeling like Vivian all over again. I couldn't lose the woman I loved so deeply again. So, I never looked. I had no need to. Plus, Evette came back around. I chalked everything up to the stress of her career.

Well, I called the guy I hired. I wanted to know what he found out. I had to if I was going to go through with marrying Evette. My conscience was eating away at me. Hiring the private investigator to look into Cam was just my way of protecting myself from getting caught up in his bullshit. And I was right to do so. I knew he was up to something the moment he showed up at my job. What he wanted was anyone's guess. Knowing Cam, it had to do with the money I earned and stored away. It was mine. Every bloodstained dollar I had earned. The problem was, Cam was every street nigga's nightmare. He was trigga happy and flashy. He wasted every dollar he made on cars, jewelry, and strip clubs. Yeah, he tricked out on the occasional chick, but for the most part, as soon as we made money, he spent it just as quick. Me stacking my money only infuriated Cam. It made sense on why he would set me up to take the fall. He thought he was going to get his hands on my millions. But that explained why I looked into Cam. Nothing up till this point made any sense about what Evette was up to.

I met up with Jeff. He was a retired detective who became a private investigator after twenty years on the force. I had already taken a seat at the coffee shop he suggested we meet at when he arrived. Jeff looked every bit like a shady detective. His unshaven face and wrinkled clothes suggested that he either rolled out of bed without giving a second thought to his hygiene or he was out all night on a stakeout. Either way, he didn't give one fuck about how he looked, and it was two in the afternoon. Jeff took a seat across from me. He waved the waitress over and ordered a steak and egg sandwich and a cup of coffee, black. Jeff slapped the dirty manilla envelope on the table in front of me.

"Are you sure you want to open that?"

"Hell no I'm not sure."

"Well, you betta be sure. Because once you do, there is no going back."

Jeff was right. I didn't need an envelope to tell me that Evette was doing something behind my back. I might have done a few years in the pen, but I knew when the fuck I was being played. I guess I just didn't want to believe that she, of all people, would be the one to break my heart. My gut was never wrong. I trusted it more than I trusted my heart. That intuition kept me safe all those years in prison and on the street. It was only when I let my guard down and went against my gut feeling that I ended up doing time. I didn't need anyone to tell me that Cam was behind what went down. I just didn't want to believe that someone I called my brother would do it. Just like I wanted to believe that Vivian would wait for me. Her words, not mine. And she let me down, just like my gut told me she would. Now Evette.

"I already know what's in here." As I grabbed the legal-size envelope, I stated, "I just need to confirm the who." The surprised look on my face said it all.

"You good?"

"Naw. But I will be." I said, snarling as my lip twisted up. I could feel the heat burning within me. The images of Cam and Evette. Her leaving his place. The secret meet ups. All gave me the ammo I needed. Fifteen years of anger that had been hibernating deep inside my soul woke the bear that had been sleeping. "Thanks," I said as I picked the package up and left the coffee shop.

"Aye, don't do anything stupid," I heard Jeff yell behind me.

Naw, I wouldn't be stupid. But I would have the last say.

CHAPTER THIRTY-SEVEN

Evette

I pulled into my condo parking garage. Before I could even get out of the car, a hand grabbed me from behind. I panicked and went to hit the key fob alarm to scare off whomever was trying to rob me when I heard Cam's voice.

"Bitch, the only reason you still standing is because you're pregnant. Don't make me regret not killing you."

His words stopped me in my tracks. I knew I had failed at convincing Deshawn. Hell, I didn't even try. I thought I could finagle my way out of this. But like everything I had been doing over the past few months, all I could do was try to lie my way out of this situation. "Cam, Deshawn isn't going for it."

"Bitch, you didn't even try."

"I did. I promise."

"You must think I'm one of them niggas you fucking. Where is he keeping the money?"

"He didn't tell me that. All I know is that he has it."

"Bullshit."

"No. I'm serious. We talked about purchasing a home, the wedding budget, and how much money he had put away before he got locked up. But he never told me where the money was. I just assumed it was in the bank."

"Bitch. You just can't put dirty money in the bank."

"I don't know," I yelled.

"Who the fuck you getting loud with?" He said, grabbing me by my throat. The pressure he applied to my throat was causing me to cough as my airway closed. Tears streamed down my face as I tried to fight off Cam's grip. Without warning, Cam's fingers loosened, and I fell to the concrete.

Deshawn

I pulled into the parking garage of Evette's condo. I immediately spotted Cam and Evette engrossed in a deep conversation. The rage that took over me at the sight of seeing them together took over. All I could hear in my head was Cam's voice echoing the last conversation we had when he stated Evette wasn't shit. How would he know that if he had never known her? The fact was that they knew each other. Apparently, they knew each other really well. Thoughts were racing through my mind. The images of the two of them that Jeff gave me played over and over as I put the car in park and leaped out of my truck, running over to them.

Just as I arrived, Cam had Evette yoked up. Out of instinct, I laid into Cam, punching him dead in his jaw. He instantly lost his grip on Evette. I watched as she fell to the ground. My fists connected again as he stumbled backwards. My anger wouldn't allow me to stop swinging on him.

"Nigga, I told you to stay away from her."

"Stop it Deshawn! Stop!"

The cries coming from Evette caused me to take a step back. My face hardened as my hands balled up, ready to deliver another round of punishment to Cam.

"So this what you been doing Evette?" I yelled out, causing her to jump in shock. I walked over to Cam. He was trying to catch his breath. I took my eyes off of him for just a second to look Evette in the eyes. That's when I heard the click of a gun being cocked. I turned to see Cam pointing a gun at me. My heart was already racing. This beef between me and Cam was damn near twenty years in the making.

"You better use that on me because Imma kill you nigga!"

"Over some bitch that ain't even yours?" Cam laughed.

His words hit me in my heart. "No, because you a bitch ass nigga!"

"Imma Bitch? Imma Bitch? Nigga all this could have been avoided had you just given me the money when you had the chance."

"You did all this over some money. Nigga, that money is mine. All the blood that was shed for those millions was on my hands. I earned every dime and I be damned if I sat in prison for all those years and not have anything to show for it."

"That money was ours. You took it."

"Your dumb ass spent your money. Or don't you remember? The clothes, the jewelry, the cars and all the partyin you did back them. That's where your money went. I don't have shit of yours."

"Naw. That's not how I see it. We were supposed to be family!"

"Fuck family! Was I family when you set me up?"

There was a shocked look on Cam's face. Then he grinned a wicked smile. "I didn't think you knew about that."

"Yea. Like I said, fuck you."

"Be happy it was prison and not a bullet. "

"Well, here's your chance now, Nigga. You want my money and my girl? Shoot me now."

"Don't know nobody want yo bitch but you."

I guess the look on my face gave away my internal thoughts.

"Damn nigga, you thought... Oh hell no. But the way niggas willing to die over her pussy got me second guessing my choices." He laughed. His words had me seeing red as I lunged toward Cam. We fell to the ground, and the gun flew out of his hand. We rolled around on the cold concrete. Cam landed a few punches before I was able to pin him down. My fists connected with his face repeatedly. The blood from his nose and mouth flung across my shirt and stained my fists.

"Wait. Wait.. Deshawn." Evette screamed as she tried to pull me off of Cam.

"Get the fuck off me! " I yelled as I pushed her away.

"I'm not sleeping with yo bitch" Cam uttered through his swollen, bloody face.

"Huh,"

"I'm not sleeping with Cam," Evette yelled.

I looked down at Cam's distorted face. He lay on the ground, bloodied and gasping for air. "But I saw you two."

"All I wanted was the money. She was supposed to convince you to give me the money. Or I would.."

"Shut up Cam! Deshawn, you can't believe anything he says."

"Evette stop it!" I yelled over her words.

"You beat the shit out of me and now you wanna hear what I have to say," Cam joked.

I knew in a weird way, all Cam wanted was to reconnect with me. He went about it the wrong way. Whatever he remembers about our past relationship had been gone. We weren't friends and even further from being brothers. The day I got locked up; Cam changed the dynamics of that relationship forever. All over his greed. And for what? Nothing. If he wanted to shoot me, he would have killed me already. But he didn't. And if I wanted him dead, surely he had given me enough ammo to do so. Neither of us wanted that. Despite what this nigga did to me, I wanted to hear him out. I deserved to know what the fuck was going on.

"Evette's baby may not be yours D." Cam spoke, spitting blood out of his mouth.

"What you know about my baby?" I went to lunge at him again for disrespecting Evette and my seed.

"Naw D, it ain't me. Go ask that nigga." Cam pointed over my shoulder. I turned around to see Radir rushing over toward Evette.

Evette

"Stay away from me, Radir."

"We need to talk now!"

"There is nothing else to talk about. I think you and Sharmaine have done all the talking I needed to hear."

"As long as you carrying my baby, we're going to talk," Radir commanded. His words caught the attention of Deshawn. The look on Deshawn's face broke my heart. Never in a million years did I think my life would come down to this. All the lies, sneaking around and playing games finally caught up to me. There was no way out of this. The truth was going to come out whether or not I wanted it to. I knew the way Deshawn was stepping toward Radir, he was about to unleash the same ass whoopin on him that he gave Cam.

"Deshawn no!" I screamed as his fist made contact with Radir's side profile.

"I KNEW IT. I KNEW IT WAS YOU!" Deshawn cried out loud as he repeatedly attacked Radir.

"Stop it Deshawn, Baby, please." I pleaded.

The look of hate and fury in Deshawn's eyes as he looked at me was a side of him I had never witnessed.

"You crying over this nigga?"

"No, baby. He's not worth it. I just.."

"You just what? Been fucking this bitch ass nigga behind my back. All this time I thought... I thought. Who is the father of your baby?"

The tone in Deshawn's voice scared me to my core. I shook with fear because I knew my answer wouldn't be enough for him.

"Evette, you betta start talking"

"I... I don't know."

Deshawn let go of Radir and walked toward me. "I want it to be yours. I mean, I think it's your baby," I whimpered.

"You think, or you know? How many other niggas could it be? Seems to me like you been fucking your way through the crew." Deshawn yelled in my face.

"I never slept with Cam."

"That might be the first honest thing you've said in a long time. So you and that nigga? Huh? Answer me!"

The tears just continued rolling down my face. My sobs and whimpers fell on deaf ears. Deshawn could not have cared less about my cries and attempts to calm him down. I gave in and decide to just speak my truth. If I had any chance at Deshawn forgiving me, I had to come clean.

"Deshawn, I've been seeing Radir behind your back."

"So you been fucking this nigga and me? Did you use protection?"

"Yes, but..."

"But what? All this time, I been trying to love you with every fiber of my being. I was willing to create a future with you. The whole time you been out here fucking some random nigga?"

"No. It's not like that."

"Tell me what it's like them."

"Radir is my ex-boyfriend."

"So you fucking around on me with the nigga that broke your heart? The fool that had you all torn up for years? The idiot that broke you down and left you to pick up the pieces? How funny is this shit?"

The tears kept flowing from my eyes as I stood there, hearing Deshawn's words. He didn't lie. Radir did all that, and more to me. Yet that didn't stop me from returning to the scene of the crime. I looked over at Radir, who laid there on the concrete watching all of this unfold. Cam had finally found his footing and was standing behind Deshawn with a wicked grin on his face. I wanted to kill him. I wished I could undo all the pain I had caused Deshawn. If I could go back in time, I would have left Radir right where he was in my past. But I couldn't. I could only offer the truth I had finally come to realize. "I love you, Deshawn. Baby, I am so sorry. I'm so sorry."

"You right. You sorry as fuck."

"Baby, don't..."

"Don't what Evette? All his time. I been loving you. I been faithful to you and you do this shit? I gave my heart to you, but you were too jaded to see it. This nigga damaged you so bad that you preferred to be abused then loved."

"Evette, don't listen to him. It was always supposed to be me and you," Radir chimed in.

"Nigga, you right. You both deserve each other." Deshawn stated as he started to walk away.

Deshawn

"Fuck this shit and fuck you, Evette." I stated, walking back toward my car.

"Not so fast bruh, I still need that money," Cam said, holding the gun again. I turned to see that he pointed it in my direction.

"I already told you once. I ain't given you shit. And if you point that gun, you betta use it this time."

"Don't turn your back on me, Deshawn."

"Like you turned your back on me? Go ahead and shoot me. Do whatever the fuck you think you have too, but you better kill me because I already know what I look like in orange. I ain't scared. But your ass better be ready."

Cam and I stared at each other, locked in a standoff. Memories of us as kids running the streets of Grand Rapids flashed before me. Cam was still the same small-minded child I remembered. He could never see past today and it showed the way he chose to live his life. "Pull the trigga" I dared him. The silence between the four of us was eerie. "Just like I thought." I stated as I started to walk away. That was when I heard the gun cock. I heard Evette scream my name and the loud sound of the gun going off.

BANG!

EPILOGUE

M y wife and I were strolling through the park with my son. Who would have ever thought that I would be a father? It was the perfect fall day. The rustling of the leaves on the ground and the smell of apple cider filled the air. Deshawn Jr. ran through the piles of leaves like a bulldozer. He had energy for days. Watching him have fun amused me, as his laughter played like my favorite song on repeat. We stopped at the food stand as DJ begged for a cinnamon and sugar donut. This had become his new favorite thing to ask for whenever we walked down this path in the park. My wife insisted it would spoil his appetite, but she knew I would cave and allow DJ and myself to indulge in this seasonal treat. We sat on the bench eating our treats when I noticed her.

It had been five years since I had seen Evette. Her hair looked a mess. But I was sure it was her. She wasn't wearing any makeup. Her clothing was very relaxed. But it was her. I knew her smile from anywhere. It was the only thing that resembled any memory I had of her. She was playing with a little girl that looked to be about four or five years of age. I tried not to stare. But I couldn't look away as the last memories I had of that day flashed before me.

Cam pulled the trigger as I turned to walk away. Evette had jumped up, running toward me to push me out of the way. She stepped right in front of the bullet that was meant for me. The coward tried to run, but someone had alerted the police to the situation that unraveled between all of us. Before Cam could even get in his car, the police were on his ass. They took him into custody. Radir and I attended to Evette until the paramedics arrived. Radir and I didn't say a word. Our focus was making sure Evette, and the baby were alright. When they asked who was who, I couldn't allow myself to answer. Just days ago, I would have raised my hand and loudly declared that I was her fiancé. The discoveries of the day prevented me from claiming the woman I loved dearly. I watched as Radir climbed into the back of the ambulance. The door closed behind them, and I watched as they drove away.

While Evette was in the hospital recovering, I cleared my belongings from her condo. Before leaving, I cleaned up her place and left the key she had given me on the kitchen counter. I informed my friends that the wedding had been called off. There was no need to give any details. My family and friends respected my decision and knew when the time was right, I would fill them in if necessary. Mike and Greg didn't even have much to say on the topic and work went on as if nothing ever happened.

It took me a few weeks before I could muster the courage to visit Evette in the hospital. I did call and get updates on her condition, but actually seeing her was something my heart was not ready for right away. By the time I made my way to the hospital to visit Evette, she had recovered well and was out of the intensive care unit. At first, there was nothing but silence. Neither one of us could force ourselves to speak. We just sat in the sterile room, avoiding eye contact. It wasn't until my fourth visit that we actually exchanged words. I thanked her for saving my life and she apologized continuously for hurting me. Evette confessed everything that led up to that day. I just sat there and allowed her to speak her truth.

By the sixth visit, I was ready to ask questions that had plagued my mind since that day.

"Evette, did you ever love me?"

"Yes. I did love you. I just don't think I was truly in love with you. If I'm being honest."

"Why didn't you just say that? Instead of allowing me to make a fool out of myself."

"You weren't the fool. I was. I couldn't see what I had right in front of me. I was so caught up on the idea man that I had concocted in my mind that I missed an opportunity to create something real with you."

"Why did you agree to marry me if you weren't ready?"

"I wanted to be your wife. The way you loved me, took care of me and made me feel special, I just couldn't imagine not being on the receiving end of that. I wanted so badly to give you what you wanted. Even when I pushed you away, you pushed back and loved me harder. No one ever loved me like that."

"Then why'd you do what you did?"

"I thought Radir was what I wanted. On paper he was the perfect guy. I wanted to believe that he had changed. You were the guy I needed. By the time I realized what I had in you, it was too late. I had messed up so badly."

"Is the baby mine or his?"

"I want it to be yours. But the truth is, I'm not sure. But I pray that you're the father. I pray every day for that."

Evette's honesty was probably the most transparent and vulnerable she had been during our entire relationship. It was also one of the last conversations she and I would have. The moment she asked if I could forgive her, I knew things would never be the same between us and I could not answer her question... I watched as the tears rolled down her cheeks. I couldn't bear to see her cry, but at this point, I needed to protect my heart.

We did the paternity test a month later. I waited patiently for three weeks to find out that I was not the father of her child. To my surprise, Radir wasn't the father either. It appeared that Evette had a one-night stand with one of the partners at her firm and he was the father of her child. He was married and, from what I heard, refused to have anything to do with the child. His only contribution was child support. That was the last interaction I had with Evette.

There was one good thing that came out of all of this. I found the love of my life. Bridgette had been a Godsend during the entire ordeal. She had confessed to me that she knew about the affair and had warned Evette about the consequences of her betrayal. When she found out about what happened, she checked in on me from time to time. What started out as friends just being there for each other turned into something much more. At first, Bridgette didn't want to pursue a relationship with me. Even though she and Evette weren't close friends anymore, she felt like she was breaking the girl code. But something happened between us that was so organically right, she couldn't deny what was happening.

Before I knew it, we had been dating for two years before I asked her to marry me. We had a small destination wedding, where sixty of our closest friends and family celebrated our vows with us. I must have laid the pipe damn good because Bridgette became pregnant on our honeymoon. And here we were, almost three years later, with DJ and one more child on the way.

Unlike my relationship with Evette, Bridgette knows the good, bad, and ugly about my past. My felony record doesn't play a role in our relationship, neither does the blood money I stored away for my future. She allows me to be me and to love her endlessly.

As for Cam, he is enjoying his new home in the department of corrections. He pleaded guilty to an attempted murder charge. Add in the possession of an unregistered firearm that had other bodies tied to it, Cam is doing a life sentence. He wrote me a letter a while ago, but I never opened it. I decided to close the chapter on that part of my life. I had grown and moved on. There was no need for me to read any of his thoughts or play into any of the mind games he used to keep me tied to him.

Last I heard, Evette was a single mother. Radir left as soon as the paternity test revealed he wasn't the father. I used to wish Evette had allowed me to love her. That things had turned out differently. But now I know everything turned out just the way they should have. I watched her and her daughter play. She seemed at peace. I looked away just as she caught sight of

Bridgette and me. She smiled and looked away. I turned my attention back to my family. DJ was done eating his donut. The cinnamon sugar mixture was plastered all over his face. Bridgette was taking a photo with her iPhone. I couldn't help but laugh. I turned my head toward Evette and her daughter, but they were gone. My feelings towards Evette were not negative. I wished nothing but the best for her. Hopefully, one day, she can experience the type of love I have with Bridgette.

The End

ABOUT THE AUTHOR

A.A. Lewis has lived her whole life being a creative. First as a child actor, second as a student of the arts (dance, music and theater) and now as a published author. A. A. Lewis hails from the east side of Buffalo, NY. The streets of Buffalo NY (The 716) influence many of the stories and characters that she writes about.

A. A. Lewis mixes a unique blend of street, sophistication, drama and messiness into each of her books. Her characters are unapologetic, daring, and memorable. Refusing to be stereotyped into just one aspect of the urban literary genre, her latest books, **The M.I. L, The M & M Chronicles Vol. I** and **The Dark Side of Light** showcase her range of topics and experiences of the black culture.

When A.A. Lewis is not writing, she enjoys spending time with her husband of 25 years. She has two adult sons and a granddaughter. She currently lives in Michigan.

"I write books that move readers to react. Creating complex characters that make you think, self-reflect and connect with the story on an emotional level. I want my stories to start conversations. More importantly, I want readers to have a fun. If my books don't cause you to have a reaction, good or bad then I missed an opportunity to bring you into my world"–A. A. Lewis.

Author A. A. Lewis
www.aalewis.net
lewisaa716@gmail.com

www.ingramcontent.com/pod-product-compliance
Lightning Source LLC
LaVergne TN
LVHW020411070526
838199LV00054B/3579